THE LAST BUFFALO HUNT

Also by Gary McCarthy

MUSTANG FEVER
THE DERBY MAN
SHOWDOWN AT SNAKEGRASS JUNCTION
THE FIRST SHERIFF

THE LAST BUFFALO HUNT

GARY McCARTHY

DOUBLEDAY & COMPANY, INC.

GARDEN CITY, NEW YORK

1985

All the characters in this book
are fictitious, and any resemblance
to actual persons, living or dead,
is purely coincidental.

Library of Congress Cataloging in Publication Data

McCarthy, Gary
The last buffalo hunt.

I. Title.
PS3563.C3373L37 1985   813'.54   85-12939
ISBN 0-385-23255-1

Dedication:
For Frank Roderus
Western writer and friend

THE LAST BUFFALO HUNT

CHAPTER 1

Thomas Atherton listened intently to the baying of Rutherford's blooded hounds and knew they were closing in for the kill. The hunt was almost over.

Thomas was a tall, sandy-haired young man of twenty whose growth had outstripped his ability to put on weight, leaving him lean but sharply handsome. He had high, strong cheekbones, a nose only slightly humped in spite of being three times broken—twice by horses and once by man—and feet and hands that were still too large and indicated that he was still growing. There was something about him that really did not fit in with this rural Boston gentry. Neither had his father, a crusty Scottish stablemaster who'd been just too good to fire, despite his rough manner and ways. The old man had been hell on stableboys and worse on his own son, but he could talk a horse into anything. Now, he was buried and Thomas stood in his place, unsure of both his ability and his desire to remain here instead of going out West as he'd always dreamed.

The foxhounds brought him back to the present. The rising pitch of their excited voices told him as clearly as words that the fox was tiring and its death near. Thomas frowned, thinking how the chase would end, as it always did with Cyrus Rutherford out in the lead on his powerful dapple gray hunter and the rest of the field scattered behind him. First, the handsome gentlemen who were always courting beautiful Miss Alice Rutherford and then the young, unmarried girls who could not ride like her but who wouldn't have missed the thrill of a chase that, for them, had nothing to do with the fox or the hounds.

The yelping of the dogs heightened and then, as Thomas swung about to check once again that all was in readiness for the hunt breakfast, he heard the lone gunshot. Cyrus always shot the fox before it could be torn to pieces by the hounds. It was tricky work and, more than once, he'd killed a hound by mistake or by intention, depending upon his mood. No one understood why he shot the fox. Some believed he did it out of mercy; Thomas thought otherwise. To Cyrus, the entire hunt would be a pointless exercise if the prize were ripped to shreds. Death to the hound who dared grab the red-plumed tail which Cyrus took as a trophy to tack on his stable door! It had become an after-hunt ritual for the men, and it was one that always left Thomas feeling disgusted. He wondered what Miss Alice thought about it but, of course, he was an employee and would never ask. One thing he did know, the man who married her would have to take his turn and kill the foxes, too.

Thomas' shoulders drooped a little. If Mr. Rutherford had any idea that his new young stablemaster and horse trainer actually dared to look at his beautiful daughter, he'd have run him clear out of the county.

It was midmorning. The sun was well up and already the air was hot and still. Today was going to be a scorcher. The horses used this morning would need a long walking out before they cooled. On the grassy hillside that fell away from Mr. Rutherford's white colonial mansion, the house staff had prepared refreshments. Dishes of sandwiches, salad, cakes, coffee service, piles of plates, groups of cups and saucers were all invitingly arranged. When the guests arrived, the hot dishes—curried chicken, turkey and mush-rooms, croquettes and scalloped potatoes—would be placed on the tables. Iced buckets filled with French champagne and Bavarian beer were nearby. Seated stiffly in the gazebo, an orchestra waited in heavy silence. Ranged along the food tables stood half a dozen children in maroon, high-collared livery, waving silk fans. When no one was watch-ing, they gazed longingly at the abundance before them but, mostly, they did their job of scaring away the flies. Thomas paid them scant attention as he addressed his own charges—the older stableboys who stood in polished boots and pressed trousers and jackets, poised to dash out and relieve the ladies and gentlemen of their sweating horses at the moment of their return.

All, then, was ready. Thomas began to pace back and forth in the cobbled courtyard, nervous because this was the first fox hunt of his responsibility. Over and over, he reminded himself of his father's words—he was expected to act quickly and competently yet never allow his own knowl-edge to eclipse that of Mr. Rutherford or his guests, no matter how obnoxious, drunk or overbearing they became. Only if they abused a horse could he assume a stance of authority, even then knowing he might face discharge.

"Here they come," he said, smoothing his father's coat and lining up beside his stableboys as Mr. Rutherford gal-loped into the yard, foxtail dangling from his belt.

Thomas hurried forward, grabbed the dapple gray's reins and gathered the fidgety, frothing animal under control.

"Good hunt, sir?"

"Hot, Thomas. Damned hot already!" Cyrus Rutherford climbed down, a short, gray-haired and powerful man with heavy brows, a jutting chin and a manner that radiated aggressive authority. "Everything ready?"

"Yes, sir."

"Good. I hope they've made sure there's plenty of cold drink." The tone made it clear that they *better* have done so.

Rutherford yanked the bloody foxtail from his belt and marched off toward the stables. "We'll have the shooting match at five o'clock this afternoon," he announced to his entourage.

At that moment, one of the horses suddenly chose to whirl, almost unseating its rider. Franklin Pierce, wealthy son of a Boston shipbuilder, was forced to throw his arms around the animal's neck to keep from spilling to the ground—an acutely embarrassing act, given his selfproclaimed mastery of the art of horsemanship. His reins, however, did fall and the horse, a long-legged black gelding that Thomas had worked especially hard to school, shied and bolted forward.

"Look out!" someone yelled as the runaway almost struck a lady.

Thomas was properly positioned. In two strides, he was at the gelding's side and managed to grab the bit. He could easily have pulled the gelding up short but the horse needed a lesson, so he dug in his heels and yanked hard. The black was brought around so sharply that poor Franklin was thrown heavily to the ground. He landed with a thud. They heard the breath whoosh right out of him and then he began to whoop for air.

Thomas fought the gelding to a standstill, then began to calm it as Miss Alice and her friends rushed to Franklin's aid. He was making awful gagging noises.

"Is he all right?" Thomas called anxiously, realizing he'd broken his father's cardinal rule and that Franklin Pierce was going to blame *him*.

They pulled Franklin to his feet. He was still badly shaken, and his clothes were ruined. The moment he could raise his head, he coughed, "Damn you, Atherton! I didn't need your help. I could have ridden it out. This is all your fault!"

Thomas glanced toward Mr. Rutherford, who now stood slapping the bloody foxtail against the leg of his riding breeches. The Pierce family were longtime friends of the Rutherfords.

"Sir," Thomas said, "that gelding still needs work. He might have trampled someone. But even so, it *was* my fault."

Mr. Rutherford opened his mouth, then clamped it shut as his eyes bore into Thomas. Finally, he growled, "Then work the hell out of him, Tom! Starting tomorrow. As for what just happened, I'll decide your punishment when I'm ready."

He turned to the others and his voice was edged with something very nearly like disgust. "Anyone coming to hang this trophy or not?"

The young men lurched forward, even Franklin, who was still wobbly but alert enough to hiss, "I'll see to you later."

"Yes, sir," Thomas answered, grimly determined not to smile. Miss Alice followed. She was tall, her hair was reddish blond and her eyes a deep, wonderful blue. Even under the circumstances, he admired her walk, a fine blend of grace and purpose; it reminded him of a thoroughbred filly that you just knew could run like the wind and whose offspring all would be winners.

"You needn't have jerked the animal so hard and spilled Franklin like that," she said in a low tone as she moved past, leaving her peculiar intoxicating fragrance of leather and lilac. "It wasn't at all necessary!"

"Yes, miss."

Thomas slowly expelled a deep breath. Thank God his father hadn't been here to see this. And as for Franklin Pierce . . . well, it had been almost worth it to see Miss Alice's most ardent suitor laid flat.

Thomas mounted and the black, immediately sensing mastery, lowered its head and docilely allowed itself to be ridden to the barn like a child's first horse. Thomas was smiling as he unsaddled and brushed the sweaty animal. He knew full well that, even though his father had left him almost no money, he'd passed on a gift and understanding of animals that would always earn him steady employment despite the whims of men like Cyrus Rutherford or Franklin Pierce.

"Thomas!"

He looked around. It was Carl, the farm's overseer and his immediate superior. Thomas genuinely liked and respected the browbeaten man.

"Yes?"

"One of the footmen has taken ill. You'll have to assume his place serving the champagne."

"Me?" It was unheard of that the farm's stablemaster be asked to do such a thing!

"Yes. Mr. Rutherford's orders."

Thomas' hands knotted in the gelding's mane. He understood. This was his punishment for jerking the horse hard enough to unseat young Pierce. It was to be his lesson in humility.

"Thomas." Carl's hand rested on his shoulder. "Don't say a word. Just do this and tomorrow you'll still be our valued stablemaster. If not for yourself, then out of respect for your father's memory."

He nodded his head tiredly. The nagging indecision was

back. His father was dead but he had always told him to go West if that was what he really wanted. Thomas saw nothing to gain by admitting, even to himself, that he stayed only to be near Alice.

"Here," Carl said, offering him the maroon footman's livery with its stiff shirt, buff waistcoat and white tie, "I'm afraid these are too small but you'll have to wear them anyway."

"Thanks," he groused.

Ten minutes later, Thomas was pouring champagne and perspiring copiously. The jacket bound him much too tightly across the shoulders and he couldn't breathe because of the damned tie. Alice's rich young friends congregated in the shade and, now and then, one of them would glance over at him and giggle or smirk. Thomas wished he could spray champagne into their smug faces instead of being forced to pour it like an obedient servant.

Miss Alice finally came out of the house and she was on Franklin Pierce's arm. No one was concerned enough to leave the shade, but when he reached them they all made a big fuss over him. Thomas heard his name spoken in anger. Clearly, they blamed him.

He felt his cheeks warm as he busied himself polishing glasses, endlessly rearranging the napkins and silverware. The afternoon wore on and the topic of conversation skipped over Mark Twain's new book, *Huckleberry Finn*, to the fear that America was being overrun by immigrants from Southern and Eastern Europe, to a gold rush in the Transvaal and then to the capture of the great war chief Geronimo down in Mexico.

It was this last subject that interested Thomas, because he'd followed the history of the fierce Chiricahua Apache chief's daring raids. At the time of his surrender, even the

Eastern newspapers wrote how he'd engaged no less than forty-two companies of United States Cavalry and Infantry and four thousand Mexican soldiers with only fifty starving Apaches! You had to admire the courage, the fight in such a man who'd battled so long against such overwhelming odds.

"Geronimo was a savage killer," Franklin Pierce was saying, "but at least he fought well. Last week, I went to Buffalo Bill's Wild West Show and the Indians I saw were a disgrace. They were paraded around in paint and feathers. I doubt half of them have ever been east of Albany! Probably just derelicts pulled out of saloons and dressed up in greasepaint and costumes."

"Not so," another argued. "Buffalo Bill Cody's show is authentic. Those are real cowboys and Indians."

"Don't be ridiculous. He's a charlatan!"

"Oh, come now, didn't you see them ride, rope and shoot?" someone asked.

Franklin Pierce scoffed. "I'll concede there was a measure of skill involved in the roping. But with a few months of practice, it shouldn't be very difficult."

"What about Miss Annie Oakley?" another demanded. "Anyone who has seen her or Colonel Cody shoot can attest to their remarkable marksmanship."

Franklin was ready. "They're fakes, both of them," he declared smugly. "I happened to have bribed one of Cody's employees and he admitted they use special shells filled with buckshot in their rifles and pistols. It scatters a big enough pattern to knock a flight of geese out of the sky!"

For a moment, everyone was so stunned by this revelation that nothing was said until Miss Alice coolly spoke. "If that's true, how do you explain Miss Oakley shooting the burning tip of a cigar out of a cowboy's mouth?"

Franklin blinked. Even from a distance, Thomas could see betrayal, frustration and then anger flush across his face.

"Well," she asked with raised brows, the picture of innocence waiting to be instructed, "I also witnessed Colonel Cody shooting a card turned *edgewise* out of a man's fingers. I believe that buckshot would be quite damaging to his poor assistant's appendages, would it not?"

Pierce stammered helplessly, then blurted, "Well, they're really not very good horsemen. Not nearly as good as I'd expected, given all the publicity and hoopla we've read."

Thomas could barely keep from laughing out loud. Servant's uniform or not, this was better than anything he could have imagined.

Alice saw him. *She* could tweak Franklin's overblown pride because she was his equal in every respect, but not Thomas Atherton; *he* was equal to a Rutherford or Pierce in nothing and he'd better not forget it.

"Thomas," she said in a voice sharp enough to melt the grin on his face, "what do you think of Mr. Cody's Wild West Show?"

Lacking both the time and the surfeit of money, he had never been able to attend a performance and he was too ashamed to admit it. "It looked pretty real to me."

"Oh?" Alice left the others and walked over to him. When Thomas looked directly into her eyes, he could tell she was angry. She probably had been since he'd caused Franklin Pierce that nasty spill. And now, like a true Rutherford, she was going to make him pay by making him look small, he realized.

She'd never done it before. She'd admired his father, who had taught her to ride. But Thomas wasn't his father.

He wasn't half the man his father had been and, in forgetting that, he'd left himself vulnerable at this moment of
reckoning.

"What did you think of the feats of horsemanship?" she
asked, loud enough for everyone to hear.

His mind raced in circles, trying to figure a way out of
this trap into which he'd stepped. "Good," he said, clearing his throat. "Very good, Miss Rutherford. I even compli-
mented one of their trick riders."

"How very thoughtful! Well, since you are the expert
here, I wonder if you'd do me a favor?"

"Yes, miss," he said without enthusiasm, knowing it was
impossible to back out now.

"Since you probably can fit in with them better than the
rest of us, I wonder if you'd be good enough to arrange an
introduction to Colonel Cody and Miss Oakley."

He stared at her in disbelief.

Her voice chilled. "I'm sure you heard me, Thomas. I'd
like to meet them. If Queen Victoria invited them all to
camp on the grounds of Windsor Castle during their last
tour of Europe, who, pray tell, am I not to wish to meet
such famous entertainers? Your services would be very
much appreciated by me—perhaps even by some of my
friends."

There was a murmur of assent, and Thomas felt the
noose tighten.

"I believe," she was saying, "the show goes to New York
next week, so you'll have to act quickly. In fact, I think you
should go at once and make the arrangements, don't you?"

"Yes, miss," he said, watching Franklin Pierce grin
hugely. He *knew*. They all did. This was a game and he was
the pawn set in motion for the sole purpose of amusing
them.

Thomas looked right into her blue eyes. How, he wondered, can there be so much ice inside such beauty? He managed a thin smile. "It's always an honor to serve you, Miss Rutherford. I will do my best. Good-day."

Thomas left them, though Alice had not looked especially pleased. He returned to his stable and skinned out of the footman's livery and climbed into a soft pair of worn riding pants. Then, he resaddled the black gelding and rode out the lane past the gathering of young, beautiful men and women whom he'd always aspired to join but never could. Now, they mocked his passing. Miss Alice Rutherford raised her glass in a token salute, but he looked away from her toward Boston.

Maybe, he thought, I will just keep riding and become a horse thief. And if I am caught before I reach the West, then my death will be on her conscience all the days of her life, and that would serve her right.

CHAPTER 2

He rode into Boston and had no trouble at all finding the park where Buffalo Bill's Wild West Show had camped. The Colonel encouraged the public to browse about his encampment and meet the cowboys and Indians, so Thomas eagerly plunged into this exciting new world. He saw a cowboy practicing twirling a rope and an Indian who spoke perfect English signing his autograph for a pack of wide-eyed kids. In one big, high-sided corral, a herd of long-horn cattle bawled and slung about their great racks of horns. Thomas couldn't imagine lassoing one of those monsters, much less doing anything to it. At another corral, people stood gawking at a dozen buffalo that made the longhorns seem puny by comparison. Standing nearly six feet tall at the shoulder, the huge, shaggy bulls were twice the weight of an average horse and magnificent-looking.

Thomas was entranced and studied them closely. He'd never seen real buffalo before and knew they'd become almost extinct. They had wary little eyes he knew weren't even as farseeing as his own. In this heat, the animals were shedding hair in big felt-like patches and several were rubbing themselves against the stout corral hard enough to make it rock. He noted that all of them were plagued by swarms of flies and gnats and, since their stubby little tails were woefully inadequate, they methodically pawed the earth, raising big clouds of dust that made them snort and stomp.

Grunting, pawing and rubbing, they were fascinating creatures even in captivity, but Thomas could not help but regret he'd never witnessed them running free by the millions or heard the great thunder of their hooves as they stampeded across the prairies, rolling like a muddy river flooding its banks. He'd read about the buffalo hunters, the staggering waste of their slaughter and how their big rifles had glowed red and hot with the killing. He'd read, too, of the Indians hunting them on horseback with bow and arrow. Seeing them now, Thomas couldn't comprehend anything as enormous as a buffalo being taken down by a flint arrowhead fastened to a wooden shaft.

These were the few survivors. Maybe the very last, saved only because they were a curiosity. I'm too late, he thought, ten years too late. What a sight they all must have been!

"They's somethin', ain't they, young fella," a rumbling voice behind him said.

Thomas swung around to confront a man the likes of whom he'd never seen. He was huge, a monstrous, gray-whiskered old bear with cheeks like ruined leather and deepset black eyes hard as obsidian. He stunk of grease, manure and his own self, and the leather outfit he wore was hard used and darkly spattered. He wore a coonskin cap and his immense feet were encased in beaded moccasins. He might have been fifty or seventy, but Thomas knew he was staring at a hunter, a frontiersman.

"You hear me or do I need to rattle your tree, boy?"

Thomas found his tongue. "I . . . heard you. Yes, sir, they *are* something," he managed to say.

The old giant nodded, walked over to the corral and

draped his massive forearms across the top rail. "These are puny next to some of the ones I used to shoot."

Thomas had a hundred questions but held his silence.

"Look at 'em penned up like pigs or geese. Damn shame. Gettin' old, too. See that big old bull over yonder? He's not going to make next winter. Cody paid me two hundred dollars in gold for that one."

Thomas followed the line of his finger. He was pointing to the biggest animal in the little herd, a magnificent creature who stood with his head lowered in the dust. He did look old and tired.

"You found these?"

"Yep. Didn't do 'em any favors, though. They don't look half so good penned as they did free. Then, nothin' ever does." He spat a stream of greenish yellow tobacco a good twenty feet.

"Where?" Thomas asked.

"Where what?"

"Where'd you find them?"

"Why you want to know?" The man rolled against the fence and studied Thomas.

"No special reason. I just heard they're all gone."

"Probably. Not necessarily." He began to chew. "To answer your question, I found these out in Wyoming. There's a few secret valleys left. They came outa one of 'em."

"How'd you do it?"

The hunter thought it over very carefully before he answered. "Easy. I just walked in among 'em—I'm part buffalo myself, as you can see—told 'em my friend Cody needed their company in his show and ended up by promising that I'd shoot 'em if they didn't foller me to the Union Pacific stockyards."

Thomas smiled. "That seems like a good way to do it, sir."

"Sir?" The man laughed and it sounded like rocks rolling in an empty beer barrel. "Hell, 'sir' is a cussword to men where I come from!"

"Sorry, Mister . . ."

"Moose. Moose Mulligan. I always been called Moose and a man could be called a lot worse things."

"That's true." Thomas glanced at the camp tents. It was almost dusk and he had to at least attempt to find Mr. Cody and Miss Oakley. Not that he thought there was any chance of their signing an autograph or consenting to be interviewed.

"You lookin' for someone in partic'lar?"

Thomas nodded. "Mr. Cody and Miss Oakley."

"What for?"

He told the hunter and, when he finished, the old giant shook his head with displeasure. "Hell, why don't you just tell 'em to go shinny up a splintery post? Young feller like you is wasting his time kowtowin' to rich folks. Go West! Swim the Platte and the Yellowstone. Climb the Rockies and live off the land until yore sap slows and yore ready to build a log cabin and sink yore roots."

He squinted down at the black gelding and his lip curled with contempt. "Most of all you need to ride real horses on a real *man's* saddle instead of a bitty old patch of leather."

Thomas colored. "This is a good horse. I'm training him myself."

"Good for what? He's too pretty for out West. Get a big, stout, ugly sonofabitch that'll pack you through snow or desert. Up mountains like a goat—or across rivers like a beaver."

"This is a blooded animal. He's worth a thousand dollars."

Moose either wasn't listening or didn't care. "No, he ain't. Not to a mountain man or an Indian or even a damned cowboy, he ain't."

"He's fast and he can run for miles." Thomas was losing his patience. He *knew* good horses.

Moose whooped with derision. "Fast! For miles! You want to see a real horse?"

Before Thomas could answer, Moose yanked him right out of the saddle and was dragging him along as if he were a kid. Thomas looked around helplessly in time to see Mr. Rutherford's black gelding amble out of sight. Dammit, he raged, squirming mightily but not yet daring to punch this man.

"There! Lookee there at them horses," Moose ordered, dropping Thomas beside a pole corral.

He peered through the rails. The horses were nothing at all, smallish, some spotted on the rump, others swaybacked, knock-kneed or just plain ugly. They were a motley collection by the standards he'd come to expect. "What breed are they?"

"Mustangs," Moose rumbled. "Indian ponies. Them little devils will carry you to hell and back!"

Thomas was fretting about the gelding. If it was stolen, Mr. Rutherford would see him whipped and jailed for negligence.

"Well," Moose demanded, "what do you think?"

"A little small for a man like you."

"Damn good thing nobody ever told *them* so." He scowled. "You staying for tonight's show?"

"If I find my horse. Do you. . . ."

"Good. You need some educatin'," Moose said.

And that was how Moose left things. Thomas was frantic. He ran all over the camp but the black was gone. It might have gotten out of town and made its way back to Canterbury Hills Farm, but the odds weren't in its favor. No matter what Moose said, that gelding was easily recognizable as a valuable purebred and a lot of men would try to catch it and sell it as their own.

Thomas raced out into the streets of Boston, old brick streets that ran like corridors between rows of houses in every direction. He had no idea which way to go but he had to try, so he took off. Damn old Moose, anyway!

Three hours later, he dragged back, empty-handed. The huge outdoor arena was made of canvas and painted with majestic vistas of the Rocky Mountains. He could hear the crowd cheering wildly. This was one of the very first night shows, and it all had been made possible by the invention of Thomas Edison. The show was at least half over and Thomas felt like shooting himself because of Mr. Rutherford's black hunter. It would take him two years of working for free to pay off the animal. Now, Miss Alice would know for sure that he was an irresponsible boy trying to do a man's job left by his father.

Thomas felt crushed by despair. How was he going to face them all? When Alice's friends learned about this, they'd ridicule him to death and if he lost his temper and punched one—well, he'd go to jail.

As he stood outside the arena, he knew that there was only one hope of salvaging anything and that was to get what he'd come for—the autographs and maybe an invitation for Miss Alice. If he could do that much, he'd be able to lift his head from the shame.

The ticket seller was a man without a heart. No amount of talking could get Thomas in free or even at half price, since the show was half over. Thomas paid because he was desperate.

Once inside, however, his depression and fatigue lifted with the roar of a huge crowd. Thomas found a seat and gave himself over to the performance. He had no idea what he'd already missed, but he loved the wonderful spectacle of former Pony Express riders vaulting from horse to horse after a lightning-fast change of the valuable mochilla pouches containing the mail. They weren't riding mustangs either, but horses that could have competed very well on any Eastern dirt track circuit.

The Pony Express riders were chased by a wild pack of Indians whose bloodcurdling yells raised the hairs on Thomas' scalp. Their ponies were fast but still no match for the racing horses they pursued. The announcer explained that few Pony Express riders carried a gun because of its added weight and the confidence they had in the speed of their mounts.

The Deadwood Stage and its passengers weren't nearly so lucky. When the wild Indians caught sight of it careening into the arena, they forgot all about the Pony Express and went after the stage, hot with fresh excitement. Rifle smoke, arrows and feathered lances flew thicker than quail and the shotgun rider was blasted right off his seat. The Indians overtook the Deadwood Stage and then everyone was on his feet yelling as three of the painted savages jumped onto its roof and yanked the door open. There were pretty women inside! And kids!

Thomas was as concerned as anyone until, out of nowhere, a bugle sounded and the United States Cavalry came pouring into the arena and *then* you should have seen those screaming Indians turn tail and ride!

The cavalry arrived just in time. And no sooner had ev-

eryone slumped back down in his seat and the little kids
quit bawling than a whole bunch of cowboys on bucking
horses was turned loose.

Thomas was on his feet again like everyone else. Never
had he seen anyone ride like this. And to think Franklin
Pierce had actually said the riding wasn't any good! What
an idiot! The only regret Thomas had now was that there
was no time to study each performer's ride, for they were
experts. The broncos were all killers, fire-eating dirt
pounders born to romp and stomp and drive a man's backbone through his skull or pitch him halfway to the stars.
Thomas had ridden horses that bucked, thought he'd done
pretty well, too, but it was ridiculous to think he might
have matched these cowboys. Not that he'd much want to.
More than half of the twenty or so got thrown—one of
them through the fence and one other clear up into the
seats. Both were carried out on stretchers.

When the arena finally cleared, the last bronco lassoed
and taken away, Buffalo Bill himself galloped forward all
dressed in white and seated on a prancing white stallion.
Thomas saw he wasn't a young man anymore. His midriff
bulged and his whiskers and long hair were silver. Even so,
he rode a horse as if born for it and cut a magnificent
figure.

Buffalo Bill Cody swept off his hat, saluting the crowd,
and his horse reared as the people cheered lustily.

"My friends, I thank you for coming to see us," he said
in a strong, clear voice. "I hope you come again someday.
Every year our show gets better. Miss Oakley, Chief Red
Shirt, I and my entire Wild West Show have enjoyed showing you the real frontier. But don't take our word for it if
you're still doubtin'. Pack your trunks and go see for yourself. Good-night!"

He galloped out to a thunderous ovation. Thomas sat down, feeling as if Buffalo Bill had spoken directly to him, urging him to go West in search of adventure.

"You comin' to meet 'em or not," a man growled, and Thomas knew by the smell before turning that it was Moose.

"You did it!"

"What else they got to do?"

He led Thomas through the crowd, which saw him coming and opened up like the Red Sea.

Buffalo Bill and Miss Annie Oakley were relaxing in a big tent that had Persian rugs on the floor and pictures hanging on the walls. There were desks, chairs, beds and a kitchen at the far end. What would have easily been enough rifles to have saved George Custer were propped about against the furniture, thrown across the bed and taken apart for cleaning on the tables. A huge wolf-like creature growled when Moose entered but he growled back and it scooted, tail between its legs, under a bed.

Thomas held back, then was jerked inside.

"Here he is, Bill."

Buffalo Bill was still wearing his magnificent beaded Indian jacket and, in the lamplight, he looked younger. The glow hid the deep lines in his face and flattered his pale complexion. When he stood up, Thomas met him eye to eye yet felt much smaller and very humble. Cyrus Rutherford was rich; Buffalo Bill was a legend.

"Glad to meet you, young man," Buffalo Bill said, sounding rather tired. "May I introduce you to Miss Annie Oakley."

She stepped forward. She was petite, almost delicate for a woman who could hold a rifle to her shoulder so rock steady. About five feet tall, she wore a cowboy hat, a blouse bedecked with medals that were trophies for marksmanship and a short, pleated skirt. Thomas thought her attractive, but not beautiful like Miss Alice. She had long brown hair which hung in shoulder-length curls and dark, unblinking eyes that seemed to dismiss physical appearances and look right for the inner person. Thoses eyes dominated her youthful face and Thomas was reminded that her vision was judged to be extraordinary.

They shook hands, and she had the grip of a man.

"It's an honor," he said.

"Thank you. I'm afraid I can't stay and visit. I've just learned that I must leave the show for a few weeks and rejoin it in New York. But I have autographed a picture for you *and*," she added, "for Miss Alice."

"Annie has had news of an illness in her family—nothing serious, but we want to be sure."

"I understand," Thomas said, grateful to her for the autograph and hoping that it would prove satisfactory to Miss Alice.

When she was gone, Colonel Cody poured three big glasses for whiskey all around, unloosened his wide belt and kicked off his knee-high leather boots. "Moose said you took quite a fancy to our little herd of buffalo."

"Yes, sir. I did. I'd read about them, but nothing had prepared me for their size."

"They get a lot bigger. I've killed thousands larger than those outside. But they're all gone now."

"The hell they are," Moose said without anger. "If you'd ever quit all this and go back West with me to where we belong, we could scout us up a herd."

Thomas was looking at Buffalo Bill's face and, as the man puffed his cigar, the glow of its tip seemed to catch a spark in his eyes. But it quickly died and whatever Cody had been thinking passed as he said, "There's nothing wrong with fame and fortune, Moose. We can't go back. It's not the same and neither are we. We're old now. Our bones break and don't mend right. A day in the saddle would leave us stove up and we wouldn't stand up to the desert heat or the blizzards like before. It's all changed."

But Moose wasn't buying it. "The land is still raw. There's places we know that haven't changed. Old friends we hunted with, fought Indians with, trapped and swapped lies with—they're waiting for us, Bill!"

"We'll see 'em—in heaven or hell." Cody sighed. "I know that. Right along with the buffalo and free grass. Until then, I'm willing to pay anyone who can find a herd out there and bring a good bull back to me. Our lot needs fresh blood. We can't keep inbreeding much longer. A prize bull would be worth a lot of money to me."

He turned his attention back to Thomas. "You watch out or Moose will have you talked into going West with him and searching for a ghost herd of buffalo."

"Are you sure?" Thomas asked hesitantly. "I mean, I don't doubt you, but Moose says. . . ."

He held up his hand, then refilled his own glass and Moose's. "You stick around 'til this bottle is gone and you'll hear all kinds of things from the both of us. Mostly, how it was twenty, thirty years ago."

Thomas nodded. Dynamite couldn't have blasted him out of this tent.

"Drink up," Cody ordered. "You haven't touched your poison."

Thomas drank, though the liquor flamed his throat and made his stomach flop and his eyes water. He was no drinker, but tonight he was in special company and trusted they'd show him how.

Thomas awoke to a hostile world on the floor of Buffalo Bill's tent. His head felt as if it had been bottled in bond and his tongue had licked the hair off Cody's buffalo. Worse yet, he was being shaken roughly by the powerful hands of Mr. Cyrus Rutherford, over whose shoulder peered lovely Miss Alice.

"Get up, you!" Cyrus bellowed, dragging him to his feet. "We've been hunting for you since dawn and here you are, at almost noon, drunk and asleep."

Thomas felt himself being lifted bodily. His head lurched sideways in one direction, his stomach the other.

"The black returned home," Miss Alice said. "We were afraid you'd been thrown and were lying hurt out on the road somewhere. But look at you! You ought to be ashamed."

"Buffalo Bill," he stammered. "Miss Annie Oakley, I got their autographs."

"I don't care about them!" she cried.

Mr. Rutherford released him. "I've already spoken to Mr. Cody and he takes full responsibility for your condition. He also told me that you and some idiot named Moose are going West to scout up a buffalo herd for him."

"We are?" Thomas remembered nothing of the latter part of the night before.

"Yes. He says you are planning to leave today, without notice to me."

"I am?" Thomas wished all this would slow down so that he could think a minute, explain that he must have said things last night he didn't mean. "Sir, I. . . ."

"Shut up and listen."

Thomas tore the man's hands from his shirtfront. If he

was out of a job, he sure didn't need to take any of this—
not in his present pitiable condition at least.

"Do you really think you can find wild buffalo still roam-
ing out there?" Mr. Rutherford asked.

Thomas steadied himself on a tent pole and fought down
the nausea threatening to rise in his throat. Damned if he'd
admit he was a fool. "I do," he said stubbornly, "or I
wouldn't have agreed to go with Moose. Buffalo Bill thinks
so, too. He's offered big money to capture a prize bull."

"Now, wait a minute," Mr. Rutherford cautioned. "I've
a proposition for you, young man."

"Father!"

"Quiet, my dear. This is business."

Thomas straightened. He wasn't sure what was coming,
but it had interesting possibilities. He hugged the tent pole,
feeling something like a mallet beating steadily, incessantly
at the base of his skull. "I'm listening."

"You know my skill as a rifleman. I've shot big game all
over the world. Lions, polar bears, wild boars, elephants
and apes. But I've never hunted buffalo."

"You haven't?"

"No, I haven't. Twenty years ago, I was too busy making
money and there were tens of thousands of them. Next
thing I knew, they were almost extinct. I missed out."

"Father, there's no sport in killing the poor things."

He turned to her. "Sure there is," he said patiently. "If
there weren't, they'd still be out there. Besides, it's something neither I nor several of my friends have ever done
and, therefore, is worth a lot of money."

"How much?" Thomas asked, forgetting his sour stomach, the mallet beating on his skull.

Cyrus' eyes narrowed. "We'd pay five hundred each, up
to, say, fifty."

Thomas released the tent pole and stuck out his hand. "Buffalo Bill gets the largest bull, you can have the rest. All we'll need is some expense money."

"If you don't find anything, I'll expect you to make restitution."

"It's a deal."

"A deal," the rich man echoed, gripping his hand and almost crushing it before digging out a wad of bills and shoving them at Thomas. "There's one thousand dollars in advance. Now come on, Alice!" he said, trooping outside.

She hesitated. "You look terrible."

"I feel terrible."

"Can you find them?"

"I don't know. Do you even care?" he asked, certain that she did not.

"Yes," she answered. "If there are any left, I don't want it written in the history books that my father and his friends slaughtered them."

"Alice!"

"Coming, Father."

Cyrus Rutherford pushed back inside and jabbed a menacing finger at Thomas. "One other thing. You're fired, Atherton."

Miss Alice started to say something but hadn't the chance, for she was jerked out the door and out of his life.

Forever.

Thomas slid down the pole, clutching the money in his fist. It really was a blessing his dear father wasn't alive to see him now.

CHAPTER 3

Thomas stared out the train window and watched the flat
Nebraska prairie roll by like a gentle grassy sea. This, he
knew, had once been the domain of millions of buffalo.
Although the great herds had ranged from Canada to Mexico and from Georgia to Oregon, these short-grass prairies
west of the Missouri and east of the Rockies always had
been their real home. They had provided the Great Plains
Indian tribes with everything needed for survival and would
have continued to do so, had it not been for the tide of
emigrants. First came the explorers, then the hunters and,
lastly, the endless stream of wagons which had succeeded
in dividing the buffalo into what became known as the
"southern" and "northern" herds. When the telegraph and
then the Union Pacific Railroad was being constructed, the
beasts were slaughtered so relentlessly that even Moose
Mulligan himself described the scene with a sad shake of
his head. This country had been a vast, rotting boneyard.
And finally, even the bone pickers came and sold their
harvests for a nickel a pound so that nothing of the millions
remained except their dung, their wallows and an occa-
sional skinned tree whose bark had been rubbed away or a
solitary rock polished by hair and hide.

Thomas had read of the struggle of the telegraph company to keep the itchy buffalo from rubbing against their
poles till they pushed them over. They'd tried everything

and finally resorted to attaching big spikes to the poles, confident that a solution to the problem had at last been found. To the great embarrassment of the company, those spikes had proved so appealing to buffalo that people swore the big, shaggy critters lined up to use the "special" scratchers.

The corners of Thomas' mouth turned up with amusement and he wished he'd had the nerve to tell Miss Alice that story because he loved to hear her laugh. He would miss that, and the way her hair glowed in the sunshine. All the remaining days of his life, he'd hold dear her memory, knowing none could compare with her beauty, grace and intelligence. He prayed she did not marry some twit like Franklin Pierce, who wasn't worthy to kiss the soles of her shoes.

Thomas closed his eyes and leaned his forehead against the window. There still had to be some way of winning Alice Rutherford. If he could find a herd, Cyrus would pay him enough money for him to invest in some profitable enterprise and perhaps become wealthy himself. *Then* Miss Alice would consider him worthy of her hand. It seemed that they had been inching across America forever. He was not used to sitting all day and the saloon car had little attraction for him, even though Moose had warned that this part of the journey was so monotonous it was a good idea to get drunk and stay that way until they reached Cheyenne. Moose had been diligently following his own advice and maybe he was right. Day after day, the train had crawled like a snail across this immense flat green plain. All the little railroad towns, so interesting at first, now appeared tiresomely familiar. Even their citizens had a weary sameness about them and, at each stop, women and children would push on board like hungry locusts to aggressively hawk their meat, cheese and vegetables. They would start at the first coaches, the elegant Pullmans, and work their way back through first class, second class and, finally, if there was anything left, they'd grudgingly board the shabby emigrant coaches at the rear. The emigrants had little money and endured their transcontinental journey with the patience of cattle. Thomas had seen them as they sat perched on narrow wooden benches or slept on the baggage-strewn floors. Their coaches, converted cattle cars in an advanced state of disrepair, were a disgrace. The roofs leaked in storms that left their occupants cold and shivering, and missing boards in the walls formed big gaps so that dust, flying embers and insects plagued the passengers.

They made Thomas ashamed that he'd allowed Moose to talk him into riding first class. He'd even offered to exchange coaches with one old woman but she'd proudly refused, preferring to remain huddled in a dirty blanket among her own people, who spoke earnestly in a foreign tongue. A few spoke English, and Thomas listened to them during their brief stops and came to realize that they did not feel sorry for themselves, but quite the opposite. They were the *elite* of their kind, the ones who'd saved enough money to make this last journey West in the belief that, finally, they would realize the dream for which they'd left their native countries and which they'd sought in vain in the American cities along the eastern seaboard.

Thomas lifted his own chin. Compared to these people, his life had been very easy. He'd never wanted for food or shelter, and he'd always had the promise of filling his father's shoes when the day came. Trouble was, it had come suddenly and years too soon and he hadn't been ready to settle into the mold that stamped all the men who worked at Canterbury Hills Farm. Not only that, but he'd dared to think of Miss Alice as someone remotely attainable. That, most of all, had been his downfall.

As he gazed about the elegant first-class accommodations, he felt like an impostor even though he'd bought a decent suit of clothes. He didn't belong here among these successful businessmen and their families, pressed up against a velvet seat, arm resting comfortably on polished mahogany.

Thomas suspected his new suit really hadn't fooled anyone. When he and Moose first boarded this coach, the conductor had studied their first-class tickets as if hoping there'd been a mistake, that they belonged back in another car. Moose, in particular, seemed to have created an air of disapproval although, fortunately, he'd been quite unaware of it. Nonetheless, the conductor had been discreet but very firm in his suggestion that Moose bathe immediately. The old buffalo hunter had been a sight to behold in a French tub of bubbles holding up a glass of champagne. Somehow, the porter had managed to scrape the crust of dirt from his leather shirt and breeches and then had doused them with cologne.

But even after all that, Thomas still felt they were outsiders. He contented himself with the knowledge that this ride would end in Cheyenne tomorrow and that he probably carried as much money in the inside coat pocket of his new jacket as anyone else in this coach.

Besides, he'd had plenty of time to study these passengers and not all of them were gentlemen. One, an overbearing man in his early thirties named Rodney Laird, was particularly offensive. Though dapper, manicured and expensively dressed, he stayed far too long in the saloon car and then returned drunk and abusive. Handsome, but clearly dissipating himself rapidly, he had the appearance of a gambler yet he consistently lost at cards—a fact which he made no effort to conceal as he complained bitterly to his pretty young traveling companion.

That girl was possessed of a monumental patience. She kept trying to calm him, but Laird wouldn't be consoled or persuaded to stop drinking or gambling. When he left, Thomas listened to the poor girl weep and he raged at Laird's behavior and couldn't imagine why the girl would allow herself to be mistreated by such an ill-tempered lout. It was not clear if she was his wife or his fiancée but, in either event, Thomas felt the deepest sympathy. The girl was too young and attractive to cling to such a man. She had wavy dark hair and sad brown eyes and yet, despite her unhappiness, she chatted with the other passengers as though everything was just fine. She was seated two rows behind Thomas, and he would have liked to talk with her because she obviously was intelligent and well versed in many subjects. In fact, as the trip progressed, this combination of intelligence, charm and a refusal to indulge in self-pity had made her the great favorite of everyone, including Thomas, who was fascinated by her. This fascination, he came to realize, was in part due to her knack for lively conversation without ever actually revealing anything of herself and yet drawing out everyone else's life story and present circumstances. Why, the girl hadn't even given anyone her own name!

He was reflecting on this and itching with curiosity when Moose Mulligan came swaying down the aisle. Thomas hadn't seen much of him during this journey except when he'd needed money for drinking and gambling.

Well, Thomas thought, no more. They'd already spent too much on first-class seats, and Cyrus Rutherford hadn't staked him to waste it all on frivolities and cards.

"Thomas!" Moose shouted, loud enough to be heard in the caboose twelve cars back, "why don't you come have some fun instead of sitting there lookin' like a gobbler in a roomful of coyotes."

"Please sit down," Thomas said quietly. "We've got to talk."

Moose had other plans. "Hell, I can sit later, right now I'm fixing to win us a fortune at poker! Need a fresh stake. Another hundred dollars will be fine."

"We've already spent nearly half of Mr. Rutherford's money. I can't give you any more. We'll need it for horses and supplies when we reach Cheyenne."

"Don't you worry," Moose said, winking conspiratorially while the entire coach watched. "We still got plenty of money, and I'm going to make us even more before this night is over."

Thomas shifted uneasily. He needed Moose and liked him, too, but he'd be damned if he'd let the man squander all of Cyrus Rutherford's advance—an advance *he'd* have to repay if they didn't find a buffalo herd.

"I want to know exactly what you have in mind when we reach Wyoming. You still haven't told me."

Moose reluctantly slumped down beside him. "This is right comfortable. Nicer than anything I've ever set in by a long shake. We supposed to sleep sittin' up?"

"They recline for sleeping."

"They what?" he said, rocking back hard.

"Recline," Thomas repeated, pushing a lever and making his own ease back.

"Well, I'll be damned!" He crushed the lever on his chair. It almost flattened and Moose's feet went up in the air and he crashed into the aisle, slamming his head down with considerable force. He rolled to his knees and growled,

"That's a hell of a dangerous contraption." The big frontiersman rubbed his head, righted his coonskin cap and said, "I need that hundred dollars now, *pardner.*"

"Our plans first," Thomas said with reckless determination.

"I generally make 'em up as I go. You can't count on nothin' out there," Moose said stubbornly.

"For a hundred dollars, make something up."

"At Cheyenne, tomorrow, we'll buy horses and supplies and then ride north into the Bighorn Mountains, where I found Cody's herd."

"And if there are none left?" Thomas knew there might not be. Cody's buffalo had been caught years ago.

"Then we keep riding north and asking Indians all along the way."

"Why would they tell white strangers where to find the last free buffalo?"

"Most wouldn't. But a few who like the firewater enough'd tell us anything for a jug."

"Are they friendly?" Thomas knew that all the tribes had been subjugated but the memory of Custer was still young enough to cause him worry.

"Friendly?" Moose pondered the question. "I got a few friends among 'em but most would as soon shoot and scalp us as not. Thing is, they're all supposed to be on reservations, but they'd starve if they didn't go out and hunt. I figure we might run across Crow, Arapahoe, Cheyenne, Blackfoot or Shoshoni before we're done. Might take us this year and next, but we'll find one last herd and earn our pot of gold."

Thomas thought of Miss Alice. "We'll probably be rich and famous before this is over."

A shadow crossed Moose's eyes. "Money is fine but I

don't give a damn about the fame. That's ruining Cody. Now, then, how about that measly hundred dollars."

Thomas dug out his wallet and gave him the money. "It needs to last the night to Cheyenne," he advised.

Moose punched the lever on his chair and shoved him down flat. "Sleep soft, my friend, 'cause after tonight, you'll get to know the cold, hard ground."

Thomas struggled erect as Moose sauntered back up the aisle. There was no question in his mind that he and this giant were going to tangle before this was over and that he was going to come out the loser. His father had always told him that a man had to earn people's respect in many different ways. For Cyrus Rutherford to respect you, you had to have lots of money. Others measured you by your profession, your intellect or ability to handle whiskey or a deck of cards. But with someone like Moose Mulligan, you earned respect by your toughness, your grit and spit.

Thomas thought himself reasonably tough. As the son of the stablemaster, he'd had to meet frequent challenges of stableboys larger and stronger than himself. He'd learned to fight almost as early as he'd learned to ride and, though he'd been beaten, he'd never been whipped and he guessed he owed his father plenty for teaching him the difference.

He heard a muffled oath behind him and then these desperate words, "Rodney, please forgive me, but I don't love you!"

Thomas swung around just in time to see Laird's open hand blur in a tight arc that ended hard against the girl's cheek, causing her to rock back in pain.

"You're going to marry me in Sacramento, dammit, or so help me God I'll make you wish you'd never been born!"

The last thing Thomas wanted was trouble, but he couldn't ignore the pleading in the girl's eyes when she saw him spring into the aisle. In two quick steps, he was beside them and ready to fight.

"You touch her again and they'll carry you out of here," Thomas said, clenching his fists.

Laird wasn't a bit afraid. His face got ugly and he hissed, "Get out of here before I teach you to mind your own business!"

"Stand up and fight!"

Laird wasn't as tall as Thomas, but he outweighed him a good thirty pounds and there was a hard, square-jawed look about him that indicated he was a seasoned battler, a man accustomed to winning. He started to rise and his lips twisted with cruel expectancy.

"Gentlemen!" the conductor shouted, jumping between them. "The first man to swing will be ejected by force!"

To back his words, two strong black porters came rushing up and, for the first time, they were looking at passengers and they weren't bowing or smiling.

"He struck the young lady!" Thomas said accusingly.

The conductor turned to face Rodney Laird. "We'll have no such abuses on the Union Pacific, sir. Another such incident and you will be asked to depart at Julesburg—our 2 A.M. fuel-and-water stop."

"We're paid up for Sacramento!" Laird snapped.

"Your money will be partially refunded, sir, unless you behave."

Laird wanted to fight but was just sober enough to realize the conductor wasn't bluffing. He had to settle for glaring at the man in silence.

Thomas studied the girl. He'd thought her face would be swelling up but it wasn't and, except for a dampness at the corners of her eyes, she looked under control and was even bravely trying to smile. Thomas wasn't fooled for a moment. Despite her extraordinary control, she was stretched like a piano wire and on the verge of snapping.

"If you would like to join me, I'd be honored," he said to her, not giving a damn if Laird exploded or not.

"Mr. Atherton!" the conductor shouted. "Take your seat."

Thomas reluctantly obeyed, but not before the girl declined his offer with a grateful shake of her head. On his way back to his seat, the other passengers looked at him with newfound respect. He felt very good inside and proud that, of all of them, he'd been the one to take action. When he sat down, the girl's expression of gratitude lingered in his mind. He felt almost guilty because of Miss Alice.

The train rolled on. Thomas watched the sun dive into the flat horizon ahead and began to see the locomotive's sparks light the night sky. He could feel the engine working harder and knew they were climbing off the Nebraska plains. Sometime in the night, they'd pass into Wyoming and, to his mind, that was the real West—the place where cowboys and Indians lived and where cattle and pronghorn antelope grazed side by side against a sky bigger than the world itself. He felt a stir of excitement. He made himself close his eyes, knowing he couldn't sleep because, if Laird tried to hurt the girl again, he wanted to be alert enough to protect her—fast.

But he must have dozed off because, sometime in the night, he was awakened by a gentle but insistent tug at his sleeve.

"Sir," the voice whispered, "I need your help."

Thomas sat up at once. The coach was in semidarkness

but he knew at once that it was the girl. He tensed, half expecting a blow that didn't come, and then he realized that, except for himself and the frightened girl at his side, everyone was asleep.

It was her perfume that aroused and fully brought him to his senses. "What's wrong?"

"Nothing, not yet anyway, but I don't know when Rodney will come back drunk again and. . . ."

Her voice broke and she began to cry very softly against his shoulder. Thomas wasn't sure how to handle this. He patted her awkwardly and, when that didn't help, he slipped his arm around her and held her close. He'd never held a girl who smelled so good and felt so soft and vulnerable.

"Don't you worry," he said. "That man won't hit you again. Not as long as I'm around."

She quickly regained her composure and, in the soft lamplight, he could feel trust growing in her. "You're so brave and kind. I wish I'd promised to marry a man like you instead of Rodney. I'm so afraid."

"Then leave him! Go back to where you came from. You must have a family and friends."

"No family. I'm from Chicago. They all died in the typhoid epidemic we had two years ago. Mother, father," her voice caught in her throat, "even my only brother."

Thomas was speechless. My Lord, how this girl had suffered!

She closed her eyes and fresh tears dampened her cheeks. "I often wish I had died, too, and never reached out in my loneliness and sorrow to such a beast as Rodney Laird. My life . . . is ruined."

"No. Once things change and you're free of that man.
. . ."

"How can I do that!" she sobbed brokenly. "I've no money. No possessions. No one to turn to out here, where I've heard a young woman isn't safe alone."

Was that an invitation? Thomas cleared his throat. Even if it was, he and Moose had a job to do—the last thing he could afford was to get tied up with a pretty girl.

"Listen, I can give you some money. Enough to pay your room and board until you could find a job or. . . ." He'd meant to say another fiancé but caught himself in time. Still, it was obvious enough that someone as pretty as she was would be swamped with marriage offers from eligible bachelors. She'd just have to be more choosy.

"Thomas," she said, looking up at him, "you're the sweetest man I've ever known. Are you . . . romantically attached?"

He was thankful for the dimness in the coach because his cheeks warmed and when she asked him about his past, telling her about himself seemed the easiest thing he'd ever done. And she *really* listened. Thomas lost track of time as the train rolled on into the night. He told her about his father, and the mother he'd lost to a fever when he was only ten. The words poured out of him because she was the first person who actually was interested in what he considered a very unexciting childhood.

But when he got to the part about Buffalo Bill Cody and his Wild West Show, Thomas could sense her interest really heighten, especially when he told her all about Mr. Rutherford's incredibly generous offer.

"Why, you'll be rich, Thomas! What are you going to do with so much money?"

He lacked the heart to tell her how he dreamed of winning the love and respect of Miss Alice because he knew it would disappoint her.

"We haven't got it yet."

"Oh, but you will, won't you?"

"I don't know. Even Moose says it'll be hard, maybe impossible. People see a buffalo, they just naturally seem to want to shoot it. If they're upwind, buffalo won't even run. Poor eyesight was their downfall. Most everybody knows that."

"Aren't you worried that someone else might receive the same offer?" she asked. "Maybe beat you to it?"

"No. Mr. Rutherford gave me the money to find them, and Moose Mulligan is the only one who knows where there might still be a few left."

"Maybe someone has kept some *tame* ones," she ventured.

"Tame ones? For what purpose? Besides, Mr. Rutherford and his friends wouldn't be interested. There'd be no sport in the hunt."

"You said there was no challenge, anyway. How would they know the difference?"

He frowned. "They're hunters," he said finally. "They just would."

"I suppose, but . . . Rodney!"

Thomas swung around, realizing too late that he'd completely forgotten about the man. He looked up, saw the gun butt glint in the lamplight and tried to duck the blow. He failed. Orange lights flashed behind his eyes and he slumped sideways, trying desperately to retain consciousness and yet slipping ever closer toward the edge of a swirling, black abyss.

He heard urgent, whispered voices. They sounded far away, like needlepoints of starlight.

"Get his wallet, Sally."

"Don't hit him again. You'll kill him, Rodney."

"Better him than us in prison."

A cool hand slipped deftly into his inside coat pocket and Thomas groaned.

"What are you doing?"

"I'm leaving him a twenty, damn you! Hurry, we're coming into Julesburg."

He felt the brush of her lips on his cheek and her perfume filled his nostrils. Lilacs. That's what it was, and the scent touched a long-forgotten memory to which he joyfully gave himself up.

Thomas floated over the black abyss. He was in the springtime of his tenth year and the lilacs were in bloom as he walked beside his mother.

CHAPTER 4

Cheyenne was fast becoming a prosperous community, but Thomas didn't appreciate this when he arrived. With a busted head and an empty wallet, he was one of the sorriest first-class coach passengers ever to stagger into town.

But Cheyenne didn't care. Born a railroad construction town like dozens of others between Omaha, Nebraska, and Sacramento, California, Lady Luck had smiled on it for no better reason than that Cheyenne was located in just the right place to build a branch line south to the thriving city of Denver. The Union Pacific spent a lot of money building a train yard, stockyards and locomotive repair shops, and the observant city fathers knew they were in business to stay. Cheyenne easily grabbed the honor of being named Territorial Capital from its jealous neighbor to the west, Laramie, and almost immediately the citizens designated a prime piece of land for the site of the future state capital building. In the early 1870s, optimism had run high and the great cattle drives had poured men, longhorns and money into the rich Wyoming grasslands.

Thomas would learn all this later, but when he and Moose arrived they were anything but prosperous or interested in Cheyenne's past. Fortunately, Moose had a few friends, one being the livery stable owner, Pete Hammer. Pete pitched fresh straw into an empty horse stall and, outside of the flies, it was a good arrangement, all things considered. But Thomas wasn't in a very appreciative mood. He was seething inside. He'd been lied to, tricked and then robbed by a girl whose sweet innocence he'd tried to protect.

Sweet innocence? Sally Whatever-her-name-was had been anything but innocent. She'd judged him for a naive fool and then set him up for her boyfriend, Rodney. When Thomas thought about all the deeply personal things he'd confided to Sally about his past, his good childhood memories as well as the most painful ones—well, it just made the hurting even worse.

He never should have left the security of Canterbury Hills Farm, thinking he could go West and succeed. Maybe he could use his fists, but what good were they against a gun or a knife? Rodney Laird—if that was his name— hadn't concerned himself with fair play and Thomas doubted anyone else out here would either. Often, during that first week as he lay recovering, he resolved to give up and return to Boston. If Mr. Rutherford wouldn't take him back as a lowly stableboy, then someone else who knew how good he was with horses might offer him a job. In four or five years, he could repay Mr. Rutherford and maybe even rise again to a position of responsibility.

But how could he face Alice or that arrogant Franklin Pierce, who would track him down just to gloat over his failure? And there was one other reason for his final decision to stay and it was called revenge. If he remained out here, the day would surely arrive when he'd cross Sally and Rodney's path. And then, things would be a whole lot different. He'd be packing a gun and he'd know how to use either end of it.

Thomas couldn't wait.

On Saturday, Moose came bustling into the livery stable leading two fine saddle horses and a pair of heavily laden pack mules.

"Get up!" he roared. "We're in business again!"

Thomas sat up in a hurry, not daring to believe his ears. "Are they really ours?"

"Yep. We got enough supplies to track buffalo to the ends of the earth."

"But how?" It seemed too good to be true.

"A rich backer, of course." Moose squatted down beside him. "Tom, you should have heard me talk! To hear me tell of it, there's a herd of buffalo just waiting outside the Cheyenne city limits, pantin' to make us rich."

Thomas shook his head in admiration. "Moose, I got to admit it, this time you really saved us. Why, those are even good horses."

"First class. The whole damned outfit! Just like the train. We are going in style! Woo-wee!"

"How'd you find him?" he asked with a grin.

"Who?"

"Our backer."

"I didn't. He found me. Course, you understand I've quite a reputation. This fella must of heard of me back East somewheres, 'cause he knew about the deal Rutherford offered and all he wanted was equal shares."

"Equal shares!" Thomas cried. "I won't do it. Not for a thousand-dollar outfit."

Moose's eyes widened. "Are you crazy? Even if we don't find a damn thing, we still get to keep everything. This way, we can't lose."

"Yeah, but. . . ."

"But nothin'!" Moose was getting angry. "We damn sure can't hunt buffalo on foot and they hang you for stealing chickens in Wyoming, much less mules and horses. We need food, bedrolls, weapons, ammunition and whiskey for trading. This man has paid for everything."

They stared hard at each other and finally Thomas looked away. Dammit, Moose was right. They did need a big stake in a big hurry. A third of a fortune was better than nothing.

"All right," he grumbled, "tell our partner it's a deal. What's his name?"

"Nice young fella, even if he is pretty cocky for an Eastern rich kid."

Thomas' stomach tensed involuntarily.

"His name," Moose continued, "is Franklin F. Pierce."

Thomas came straight up off the ground and ready to fight.

"Damn him!" he shouted. "What's *he* doing in Cheyenne. The deal is off."

"What the hell you mean it's off!" Moose shouted. "His money is as good as the next man's. All he wants to do is mosey along."

"Never!"

Moose looked back at the horses, the packs and the mules and then said, "You're going to be awful lonesome in Wyoming. As for myself, this could be my last big chance. Pierce and I are pardners now, only question is, are you in or out?"

"Out."

"Suit yourself," Moose drawled. "Pierce has got the money, I got the savvy and I can't figure out for the life of me what you're offering 'cept a cracked head and a pair of empty pockets."

When he started to turn away, Thomas snapped, "I didn't think you'd sell out a friend."

"I haven't. Thomas, you're a hotheaded young fool that's just sold yourself out. I made Pierce this deal providing you were a part of it, and I can tell you it wasn't easy. He don't like you any better than you do him. But I hung in there like a friend and look what I get for thanks."

Moose climbed on his new horse and glowered down. "You aren't smart or tough enough for what's out there."

"And you think Franklin Pierce is?"

"He's been ahuntin' all over the world. Told me he'd even gone on one of them African saffurries and shot lions and elephants. Besides, it don't matter what he can or can't do as long as I'm running the show."

"You won't be," Thomas warned. "When he bought that outfit, he also bought Moose Mulligan."

The old hunter stiffened. "We'll just see about that, Tom. All I know for sure is this—I'm *in* the hunt and you're *out* of it. Think about that."

He rode away then, right through the double barn doors and on down the street. Thomas watched him until he rounded a corner and then he sat down and started pulling on his boots. He had no idea why Franklin Pierce had come all the way out here to earn money he surely didn't need. Franklin wasn't stupid; he'd have to realize this wasn't going to be any Sunday picnic even with the best guide and outfit money could buy.

Then why had he come? Thomas jammed his shirt into his pants and knocked the straw out of his blood-matted hair. He was a mess and he knew it, and Franklin would delight in his appearance. He'd be sure to tell Alice and. . . .

Alice. *That* was why Franklin had gone to all this trouble

and expense. He couldn't bear the thought that Thomas actually might succeed and return in triumph as a fully self-made man.

Thomas eased down, wanting to think this out very carefully. So far, he'd made every mistake possible and gotten himself into a pathetic state of affairs. But, if he was right about this, if it actually was so important to Franklin to impress Alice, then it meant something very, very good. It meant that he considered Thomas a serious rival for Alice's hand.

He smiled. By damn, he thought, I just can't give up now. The way he figured it, the stakes had suddenly been raised.

Thomas watched them ride out of Cheyenne. Moose gave no indication that he saw Thomas standing on the boardwalk as they steered their horses past a gallows whose trap door was being tested for a hanging.

Franklin was riding a showy looking palomino. He'd bought a new Western outfit—so new it was still creased along the sleeves and trouser legs. His Stetson didn't even have a smudge print, and the hatband was made of silver conchos. Thomas had to admit he cut a handsome figure. He was clean shaven, blond and could charm a snake. He used big words and dropped names like crazy, but now he still looked like just what he was—a young rich man out for a good time but with no real idea what he was in for. However, Thomas mused, neither do I, if I go out into the wilderness. Without Moose, I'll probably get lost, scalped or eaten.

As the unlikely pair rode down Central Avenue toward the railroad tracks, people stopped to admire their fine horses and saddles, mules and packs. Franklin wore a revolver on his hip and its carved holster squeaked. Poking out of his saddle boot was a big buffalo rifle just like the one Moose was shouldering proudly. In his rugged, competent hands, the weapon looked right; in Franklin's, it would appear ridiculous.

Thomas' fists knotted at his sides, and it was an effort not to run out and drag Franklin from his saddle and knock that smug look of arrogance off his aristocratic face. Out here, people said your name and background didn't count, that men were equal until they faced trouble and only then were they judged. Thomas sure did hope so—all his life he'd had to bow his head and scrape before rich, powerful men and their snooty children. Now, the rules were different but, watching this pair ride off, it sadly occurred to Thomas that he was still on the losing end of this game called "have and have-not."

He twisted away, not wanting to think about how pitiful his chances were of finding a herd of wild buffalo before Moose and Franklin. Thomas slowly moved over to a big horse trough. He knelt in the dust and plunged his head underwater. It felt good and cold. Senses and purpose cleared, he combed his hair, slapped dirt from his knees and headed for the nearest saloon. If he could pour chilled champagne for the likes of Mr. Rutherford and his fancy guests, he danged sure could pour bad whiskey for a room full of hell-raising cowboys.

It had been easy to get a bartender's job once he'd been able to convince the owners he did not drink. As a teetotaler, he was instantly valuable and bartending suited him fine. In one week, he learned more about Cheyenne than half its longtime citizens. This was cattle country, as fine as there was anywhere in America. Over at the famous Chey-

enne Club, wealthy cattle barons mixed with English no-
blemen to form the most powerful organization in the territory, the Wyoming Stock Growers' Association. Thomas
never saw any of that kind. The Pioneer Club catered to a
working man's crowd, soldiers from the army fort nearby,
cowboys and shopkeepers. It wasn't the best saloon in
town, but it was a long way from being the worst and the
tips were generous.

At the end of his first week, he'd saved thirty-three dollars in wages and tips by outworking everyone and not
drinking or gambling his money right back into the till. He
constantly asked questions of anyone who'd gone north
into the Bighorn Mountains or beyond. From one old fellow for whom he'd bought drinks, he got a map of the
country to the north showing the rivers, mountains and
valleys along with any small settlements and sites of possible Indian encampments.

He learned that, a few years back, gold had been discovered in the Black Hills of Dakota and thousands of miners
had rushed off to make their strike. Thomas knew there
was no chance of any buffalo having survived in that direction. The more he listened and asked, the more he realized
that no free-roaming buffalo had been seen since a decade
before, when the hiders had swept them from the plains.

"But," he argued desperately, "there must be a few left
somewhere."

"Maybe, way north."

"How far?"

"Canada or beyond, where the ground never thaws. Now
pour me another drink and I'll draw you a map of the
Wind River country."

Thomas had poured and had gotten the map, though his
spirits plummeted. He tried to remind himself over and

over that someone as knowledgeable as Moose Mulligan wouldn't have gone out searching if there wasn't some possibility of finding buffalo.

He was telling himself that very thing one morning as he hurried to work, knowing the afternoon's hanging was going to make this a brisk day for business. Thomas found the crowds and excitement depressing. Why anyone would want to watch some poor devil swing and kick at the end of a rope was a mystery. But there was no mistaking the way the town had filled up for the event. He'd even had to give up his own quarters at the livery stable for the hayloft, where heat lay like a wool blanket and sleep was almost impossible.

They'd be gone tomorrow when the funeral and burial took place. Almost no one stuck around for that part.

Thomas was rounding a corner, pushing through the excited crowd, when he collided with a smallish individual in a slouch hat and knocked him flying into the dirt. He quickly bent to help.

"Excuse me, I guess. . . ." The words died on his tongue. The person was frantically cramming watches and wallets back into his overcoat pockets. Before Thomas could react, the pickpocket scrambled up and was off to the races.

Thomas blinked. That face, that. . . .

"Sally," he bellowed, leaping after her, "you come back here!"

She was faster than a fox and darting through the crowd so expertly he knew she'd done it before. But Thomas had legs six inches longer than hers and nothing was going to stand between her lovely neck and his outstretched hands. Sally held her own until they broke into the open and sprinted down an alley. Out of the shadows lunged a huge dog, and the girl yelped with pain as it sank its teeth into her heel. Off balance, struggling to free herself, she crashed into a barrel and fell heavily, giving Thomas valuable seconds. He saw her climb to her feet and break free long enough to send a boot crashing into the dog's face. It howled with pain and lit out with its tail between its legs and Sally right on its heels.

He tackled her as she was sprinting across the schoolyard at Nineteenth Street. He wrapped his long arms around her knees and pulled her down. She fought like a cat. Her fingernails raked his face and her knee doubled him up in agony. Somehow, he hung on to her coat as she struggled to tear free and escape. With a desperate effort, he swung her down so hard the breath blew out of her and he did what he'd never believed any man should do—he slapped her fingernails away and bashed his knuckles into her jaw.

She collapsed like an empty bag.

It was a few minutes before he regained his wind and could stand. He clenched his teeth, then slung her over his shoulder.

She didn't weigh much more than a bale of straw or a sack of oats. Pound for pound, he'd never fought anyone or anything to compare.

"You didn't even need Rodney," he growled, heading down Carey Avenue toward Pete's livery stable.

No one gave him a second glance, assuming he was carrying a drunken friend or a whipped enemy. Even if they had thought he was toting a dead man, they wouldn't have bothered, not with a hanging drawing near.

Thomas took Sally out back near the corral and removed that old coat. It had huge pockets just crammed with jewelry and money. She was amazing. If he hadn't been a victim himself, he would probably have admired her nerve and skill because she obviously had miles of both. But he *was* a victim, and she'd robbed him of pride as well as Rutherford's stake. Because of her, he was in Cheyenne and Franklin Pierce and Moose Mulligan were out hunting his dream. She'd ruined his life and he felt no mercy.

He picked her up and her eyelids fluttered. She was waking, but he was going to speed up the process. Without ceremony but with great satisfaction, he tossed her right into the water trough.

She sank for a moment, then came up hissing and spitting, but he was ready and damned if he was going to let her climb out and kick or knee him again.

"Thomas!" she cried, wiping her eyes clear and slamming her soggy hat into the horses' water. "I should have known it was you! I've been looking for you all week."

He laughed, but the sound of it was harsh. "What kind of fool do you think I am! You set me up for Rodney. Stole my money and let him almost kill me."

She gripped the sides of the trough and looked up at him, eyes begging him to understand. "I didn't have any choice and I never meant him to hit you that hard. I was so scared, I ran."

"Liar! You're a pickpocket. A common thief."

"A thief, yes, but I swear on the Good Book I wasn't a willing one, Thomas."

He was surprised she even remembered his name. How many others had she lied to, maneuvered into telling their deepest feelings and then let old Rodney brain them?

"Let me up, please. I'm starting to shiver from the cold."

He grabbed a handful of her shirtfront and, suddenly realizing what he'd gotten ahold of, let go fast.

Sally's eyebrows rose. "You're a gentleman, Thomas. Even after all I've done, you're still a gentleman."

She was wearing a man's work boots and baggy trousers as part of her disguise, but with that soaked shirt plastered to her chest, Sally wouldn't have fooled a toddler. Thomas grabbed her belt and hauled her out of the trough and dropped her in the mud.

"Get up," he ordered, "I'm marching you straight to jail."

She shivered even harder as she climbed to her feet. She looked awful.

"That'd be a terrible injustice. Rodney made me do all those things. He threatened to kill me if I didn't."

"I don't believe you." He gave her his clean handkerchief and let her dry her face and clean the mud off her hands.

"It's the truth. I *was* deathly afraid of him. I really needed your help that night on the train. I was supposed to wait until we neared Julesburg and then go to you at the last minute, but I came earlier because I could see you were brave and kind. That you were the only true gentleman I could turn to in my hour of need."

He couldn't meet her eyes and he had to work the anger back into his voice. "Bet everything you told me was a lie. I'll bet your family never died of typhoid. You probably never even lived in Chicago."

She sniffled. "Did, too. No matter how desperate things were, I wouldn't ever make up such a foul lie. It might be a curse on my soul. I just wanted to be free of him. That's why I'm in Cheyenne instead of Julesburg. I came searching for *you*, Thomas."

"Why? You got all my money—and half the rest of the town's," he added with disgust. "And their gold watches."

"I needed money to pay you back so you could go look for those buffalo. Maybe find them and become rich."

He had to smile because her story made sense but for all the wrong reasons. A devil woman like Sally wouldn't be able to resist putting a young, soft-hearted fool like himself in her debt. She'd wrap him around her little finger.

Thomas frowned. The jail would be overflowing tonight with drunken cowboys, and he couldn't stomach the idea of little Sally in there among them.

"Well," he hedged, "I'll have to at least turn in the watches and wallets."

"And make Bob Tingsley even richer? Don't talk crazy. There's no way to tell whose wallets they are. And those watches, Thomas, Indians purely *love* watches. They'd tell you most any of their secrets for a real gold watch."

"You're unbelievable," he said, irked because he knew he was going to let her off scot free.

"I want to go with you and Moose." Sally placed her hand on his shoulders. Even wet, she was irresistible. "If you'll just get out of Cheyenne this minute, I'll do anything you ask. We can buy what we need in Laramie."

"What's your hurry?"

"Rodney. He'd shoot me for certain because he's so jealous. Please, Thomas!" She was pleading with desperation and he knew there was no way it was an act. The girl was scared.

"Moose is gone." He quickly told her the whole story and, by the time he had finished, she was pulling on her coat and begging him to go, saying, "We can borrow two horses and be gone while everybody is in the square."

He weakened. "All right," he said finally, "but I'll leave money for what we take. I know the liveryman and Pete is my friend. We'll pay him fair—no need for *us* to hang."

She paled and nodded weakly as she crammed money into his hands. "Just hurry up! I know he's close about, probably drunk and crazy to kill us both."

"I'm not afraid of him."

"You're not even armed!"

She had a very good point. Up to now, he hadn't had enough money to buy a gun and holster.

"Please, Thomas. Buy us his two best horses and saddles and let's get out of Cheyenne before Rodney finds us!"

The almost hysterical urgency in her voice shook him up and settled the matter. Thomas knew exactly which horses were for sale and which pair he wanted. He might be a greenhorn in most things, but horses were horses and these two matched sorrels were a pair that would run like the wind. Together, they saddled and bridled the horses in no time at all. He scribbled a note and left two hundred dollars and a gold watch where Pete couldn't miss them, and they mounted up.

"Not that way. The gate's locked in the back. We have to go out the front."

Sally lashed her horse and it bolted for the street. As she flew past, he thought he saw tears in her eyes.

Down the road they galloped and, with a cry, Sally reined hard at an intersection to avoid the terrible spectacle of a condemned man climbing up his own gallows.

Sally glanced back and then raced out toward the prairie, whipping her horse as if Satan himself were on her tail.

And maybe he was. For, as Thomas swept past, his heart missed a beat—the man they were hanging was Rodney Laird!

CHAPTER 5

Thomas was stunned, then outraged. She'd done it again—lied, cried and then apple-pied him into believing her tale of sorrow. It was damned clear now that Sally wasn't capable of telling the truth. She'd *known* it was Rodney who was walking that gallows, and you don't shed tears over someone you don't care about. For whatever reason, she'd used him once more and now the only real mystery was why he didn't just rein his horse toward Cheyenne and go back to work at the Pioneer Club. If he did, he could learn exactly what Rodney had done and if he'd had an accomplice—a smallish one dressed in men's clothes.

It chilled him to think that she was not only a thief but perhaps also a murderess. He let her ride on ahead, preferring to stay back where he could watch her as if in doing so he might actually fathom the truth. But it was tough. On a horse, against the backdrop of the prairie, she looked pathetically small, even wearing that sloppy army coat with the oversize pockets. Her shapeless slouch hat was pulled right down to her ears and, with those big old boots probably half stuffed with wet paper, she evoked the long-forgotten memory of an orphan he'd seen years ago early one snowy morning on Tremont Street. Everything the boy wore obviously had been stolen from the drunks passed out in Boston Common. It was funny how a memory like that just stuck in your mind. Thomas knew that the expression

he'd seen on Sally's face when she had glanced back at
Rodney would become indelible, too. That was good. He
was in love with Alice and she was a lady, while only God
Himself knew what Sally might be. He'd need to watch her
constantly, never let his guard down for a minute or she'd
charm him with her pixie smile, her damned lies and tears.
She knew every woman's trick and she'd learned them very
young. Thomas figured he was no match for her and that
he'd do well to turn back now, before it was too late.

Pride, however, wouldn't allow it and so they rode West
hour after hour, skirting the Union Pacific tracks. Sundown
found them nearing the crest of the Laramie Mountains
and watching a locomotive struggle up the grade like a
captive beast, looking as if it might blow up or just squat in
its tracks and die.

At the divide their horses needed a breather, so they
loosened the cinches and watched the sun empty itself like
a bucket of molten gold across the rim of the world. Sally
was lost in her own thoughts, and her puffy eyes were evi-
dence that she'd been crying for hours. In spite of himself,
Thomas felt sorry for her and guessed she was wondering
what price Rodney or any man would pay for one last sunset like this at the hour of his death.

When the sun finally dove into the distant range of
mountains, Thomas said, "Let's ride. Those lights out
there must be Laramie. We can find a stable and a couple
of hotel rooms. Tomorrow, we'll buy our supplies and strike
north."

She didn't answer, just cinched up tight and stepped
into the saddle. Ignoring his earlier vow about not turning
his back on her, Thomas led off through the trees. Sally
obviously wasn't capable of hurting anyone but herself today. She'd be dangerous starting tomorrow.

They found rooms, and he waited clear 'til eight o'clock the next morning before she came down for breakfast in the hotel lobby. Her eyes were dark with fatigue and her color was poor. If anything, she looked worse than the day before and Thomas thought her in no condition to undertake a trek that could last for months.

"I can go anyplace you can," she told him at the breakfast table. "In fact, I'm worried about you."

"Me!"

"That's right. I've lived out here long enough to know the dangers, which is a lot more than you can say. There's one more thing I think we ought to get straight. I want half the buffalo money."

"Half!"

"Yes."

"Does that take into account what you already stole?"

"Certainly," she answered. "I'm no crook. Besides, I'll earn my way, and then some, by the time I've led you all over Wyoming, maybe even Idaho and Montana."

"Have you ever even been there?"

"Of course!"

"Sally, the truth this time."

She stirred her coffee. "All right, I haven't. But that doesn't matter because men are men."

"What is that supposed to mean?"

"It means that, red or white, I can make them tell me things you can't. Is that plain enough?" she asked with defiance.

"It sure as hell is." He wanted to choke her. She was no good. Nothing but poison. "Won't me being along sort of cramp your style?"

"We'll just tell everyone you're my brother."

He didn't like that idea at all but decided this was no place to get into a big argument.

She carefully counted out money and shoved it to him across the table. "You do the paying, Thomas. It's the man's job."

And that was how they handled it all morning going from store to store. Sally picked their supplies then doled out the money to him, penny by penny. It was humiliating but he had to admit she knew what she was doing. They bought only what they needed, and he had to almost beg her to buy him a used Colt .45 Peacemaker and holster at the gunsmith shop. Besides that weapon, she bought them an old but serviceable .44-caliber Henry repeating rifle with a shiny brass receiver and a fifteen-shot tubular magazine. In the words of the gunsmith, "Ma'am, this honey will shoot the eyes outa a termite at a hundred yards!"

There was one other thing besides ammunition that Sally purchased and that was a fine little Remington Vest Pocket .22-caliber derringer.

"Now this one, ma'am, is almost as pretty as you," the gunsmith proselytized. "Guaranteed to hit a well at five feet."

Sally actually smiled, but the casual way she inspected and loaded the pistol again made Thomas realize how dangerous she really was. Yesterday, she'd begged him to leave Cheyenne, saying she'd do anything for him. Today, there was a warning look in those dark-circled eyes that told him *she* was capable of anything.

Only when it came to buying a pack animal did she allow him to make the choice, and then she haggled price for almost thirty minutes.

By the time everything was ready, it was nearly five

o'clock and there wasn't much more than a couple of hours of daylight remaining.

"Why don't we just stay overnight and get an early start in the morning," he offered, thinking an extra night in a real bed might be good for her.

"Do you think Moose or that Pierce fella will be making camp two hours before dark?"

"I doubt it."

"Then how can we? I'm not buying all this stuff to have a good time. It's our investment and there's no payoff for second place."

So they rode out of Laramie and cut north. The first night, they camped at the base of the mountains and ate tinned sardines and crackers, each watching the campfire from opposite sides. Thomas thought of Alice, how she looked and smelled, the way she laughed and how she could handle a horse better than Sally, who was a pretty fair rider.

He wondered if Alice was thinking of Franklin Pierce and if Sally was thinking of Rodney. One thing certain, neither of them was thinking of him. There'd been a few girls who had, though. One in particular had loved him, and she'd been pretty, too. But for some reason, he just hadn't been able to get very excited over her and he'd let her go. Maybe it had been because he'd seen Alice nearly every day and, at nineteen, he'd just not been willing to settle for second best.

He still wasn't. Oh, he had to admit he'd felt something stir inside for Sally that night when he'd held and comforted her on the westbound train, but that feeling had sure proved to be an illusion.

Now, as he stared through the flames at her, his frown dissolved once he saw she'd fallen asleep propped up against the sheepskin lining of her saddle. Damn, he thought, she is a pretty thing and I can't believe she's a murderess. A thief, yes, but not a murderess.

Her blankets had fallen from her shoulders and the night held a chill. Thomas rocked to his feet. She didn't need to catch pneumonia as the night got even colder.

He was halfway around the fire when her eyes flew open and the derringer stabbed out of the blankets, cocked and ready to fire.

Thomas froze, one foot up and one down.

"Stop right there," she hissed, "and go sit down across from me or I'll shoot you in the knee."

His anger flashed. "I was only going to cover you back up!"

"I'll just bet," she said, obviously not believing him. "Well, from now on, you just worry about yourself and leave me to do the same."

"I will," he stormed, "and that goes both ways!"

He kicked his saddle over and lay down to stare at the cold, black heavens. In addition to not trusting her, Thomas was beginning to dislike this girl intensely.

For the next two weeks, they hardly spoke to each other. They just grunted. Thomas developed a real appreciation for how much two people could communicate with grunts. They could be developed into a whole vocabulary and he was certain that, if pigs were as smart as farmers said they were, no doubt the beasts carried on pretty fair conversations.

They crossed the mighty Platte River at the place called Mormon Ferry. Day after day, they rode through the waving buffalo grass. Occasionally they saw a ranch and, once in awhile, even crossed the path of a cowboy. Whenever that happened, Sally would be transformed into a laughing, smiling girl and he was her brother. Together, they were supposed to be searching for their dear old uncle, Moose Mulligan, and Cousin Frank. Had anyone seen them? No. Then had they seen any buffalo in the past few years?

The answers were always the same, and that made Thomas edgy. What if Moose had had some specific place in mind where he felt pretty certain he could find a herd? If that were the case, then he and Sally might just as well quit this hunt now and go home—except neither one of them had a home.

A hard day's ride beyond the Powder River, they met a cowboy who'd seen a half dozen Indians riding up into a nearby canyon. He guessed they were going into the Big Horn Mountains to hunt deer or bear, both of which were still plentiful in the mountain meadows.

"Do you think there could be any buffalo up there?" Thomas asked.

"Buffalo?" The cowboy was a short, redheaded man with a brawler's scarred face. "Well, it don't seem likely, but then anything is possible. If I was a buffalo, I'd summer up high and stay close to the trees. Buffalo's got a lot of mountain billy goat in him, you know."

"Is that right?" Thomas had never heard such a thing before.

"For a fact!" the cowboy said, cocking one leg around his saddlehorn. "Same kind of kinky hair and little beady eyes. Tails are longer is all."

"Hmm," Thomas mused. "I never thought of it that way."

When the cowboy was looking at her—which was almost all the time—Sally appeared as innocent as a lamb. But when he glanced away, she rolled her eyes heavenward.

"What tribe?" she asked sweetly.

"I don't know. Probably Sioux. They were a mile or so off when I saw 'em and that was close enough. Maybe the same bloody devils that scalped Gen'ral Custer an' his troops."

Thomas felt his hair prickle.

"Thing is," the cowboy drawled, "once an Indian takes a trophy scalp, he's a renegade. He'll do it every chance he gets."

"That's nonsense," Sally clipped. "Come on, Thomas. Let's go find them."

"You're both crazy," the cowboy yelled as they rode off. "They'll do worse than scalp a white woman."

Thomas glanced sideways at Sally; her face was pale under the broad slouch hat.

"Can you even speak Sioux?" he asked quietly.

"Of course I can!"

Thomas wanted to believe her but it wasn't easy. This girl would steal the glass eyes off a blind man if there was money in it; she'd lie as easy as telling the truth. But no one was stupid enough to go riding up some narrow canyon after a band of Indians who'd fought at Little Big Horn.

Nobody.

The day grew long and the trail steeper. Fresh tracks of unshod Indian ponies were everywhere, and Thomas was afraid there was a whole lot more Sioux than the cowboy had seen. Their own horses had a difficult time of it and, by nightfall, they were stumbling with weariness.

They chose to camp in a small grassy enclosure ringed on three sides by pines and boulders and on the fourth by a pretty stream. It was sundown and trout were snapping at mosquitos, but Thomas and Sally were both too weary to fish and cook so they gnawed on some jerked beef and cold biscuits and then fell asleep listening to the wind playing music through the pines.

Thomas awoke to the aroma of fish frying. He scrubbed his eyes and yawned. "You should have gotten me up to go fishing."

"I know, but you looked so worn out last night I hadn't the heart. Besides, I always did enjoy fishing early in the morning."

She handed him a plate, knife and fork. "Eat hearty," she said, "this could be our last meal."

"If that was supposed to be funny, it wasn't." Thomas filled his plate. "We can always ride back down the trail," he said hopefully.

"It's a little too late."

"What do you mean?"

"Just that we've invited them for breakfast this morning. There's not even a breeze in this canyon, and they'll follow our smoke."

Sally speared a mouthful and ate it hungrily. "They'd better hurry or these trout will be all gone."

Thomas had lost his appetite but forced himself to eat, knowing he'd need his strength before this was over. He'd have given anything if, instead of this girl, he was sitting across from Moose Mulligan. Moose would know how to handle these visitors or if it was time to run.

"Here they are," she said in a calm voice, "across the meadow right behind you. Seven of them."

Thomas swallowed drily. They were warriors and they weren't smiling. Each carried a rifle and looked as if he knew how to use it.

Sally took a deep, steadying breath. "Now, smile and raise your open hand. I think that is the sign of peace."

Thomas stared at her. "What do you mean, you *think?* You speak their language!"

The grin on her face slowly cracked, like mud in the sun. "I'm afraid that isn't entirely true," she whispered. "I've never even met an Indian."

Thomas wished he had the time to strangle her but there just wasn't any. "You've really done it this time," he whispered, rising to his feet. He was wearing his own gun, but he might as well have left it in his saddlebags. Their only hope was in making peace.

As the Indians approached, Thomas couldn't help but admire how beautifully they rode. Even at a walk, he could tell that these men were exceptional horsemen; they gave the impression of forming that rare man-horse union that few whites ever achieved.

The Sioux were dark, handsome men, brown or sorrel like their horses. Their hair was long and all of them wore either a sweat-stained bandanna or a hat much like Sally's. Their attire was a combination of army uniforms, tanned leather and bright shirts and sashes. Some wore boots, but most had on beaded moccasins. They were taller than he'd expected, though the one in the center of the approaching line was squat and powerful, with the scar of an old sabre slash cutting from his eyebrow to the point of his jaw. He rode proudly and would have been the focus of attention anywhere in the world.

"Peace," Sally called.

"Peace," Thomas echoed, praying they understood.

The Indians reined up. Their eyes inspected every inch of the camp, and though Thomas and Sally kept saying "peace" they gave no sign of acknowledgement.

Scarface finally dismounted and approached. He moved

like a cat, sinewy and smooth. At ten paces, he halted and studied them for almost a full minute.

"Peace," he grunted.

Thomas sagged with relief and Sally began to chatter all kinds of welcoming nonsense until she realized that the Indian wasn't paying her any attention but was waiting for Thomas to make a sign or gesture.

Thomas thumped his chest with a closed fist. "Me friend!" he declared.

"Me friend," Scarface repeated, thumping his own chest.

"This my sister." He looked to Sally for help but got nothing. "Sister."

The Indian nodded. He, too, pointed to Sally. "My sister," he echoed.

"No, no. *My* sister."

"My sister." The Indian repeated gravely.

"Thomas, will you quit the sister business and ask him about buffalo!"

"Have you seen any buffalo?"

The Indian stared back vacantly. It was becoming painfully obvious that he neither spoke nor understood English. Thomas, however, had to keep trying. "Buffalo. We hunt buffalo."

Still no reaction.

Sally couldn't contain herself another second. "Buff . . . a . . . lo," she enunciated heavily, putting a fist to each ear and then pulling her hands upward in an arcing motion. "Buffalo!"

The Indian looked back at his companions, said something in his own language, then again faced Sally. "You buffalo?"

"No. Not me!" Sally cried desperately. She thought a

moment, then dropped to the earth on all fours. She lifted one cupped hand and made a pawing motion, then pretended to eat.

The Indians gaped, then looked at each other once again and shrugged.

"Dammit!" Sally cried in exasperation. "Thomas, get down here and help!"

Thomas refused because all Sally was doing was making a fool of herself. He had an idea of his own he thought might work. "Buffalo," he repeated, moving around Sally, bending his knees as if on a horse. He extended his left arm and pretended to grab a bow while, with his right, he cocked two fingers as if pulling back the string.

Taking aim with the imaginary arrow, he shot Sally who, by now, understood his game and rolled over, kicking as if mortally wounded and making what she thought were the sounds of a dying buffalo.

The Indians finally cracked. Their faces were contorted with laughter. After what seemed an eternity, Scarface was able to point down at her and nod vigorously.

"Buffalo," he said, nodding. "Buffalo! Buffalo!"

Sally climbed to her feet and she was furious, but Thomas ignored her in his excitement. "We want to *find* buffalo!" He shaded his brow and pretended to gaze off into the distance.

The show over, the Indians began to talk animatedly among themselves. Every now and then, one would point up higher into the mountains but, invariably, his hand would be knocked down in violent argument.

At last, Scarface barked something that made the others fall silent. He then launched into a passionate speech which finally ended to the accompaniment of nodding heads all around.

Thomas sighed with relief. "They understand," he said, "they *know* where the buffalo are and they'll show us."

As if comprehending his words, the Indian nodded vigorously once more, then extended his hand, palm up. "Money. Want money."

Sally snorted. *"Now,* I feel better. Before it was too easy. These people aren't going to just take us to the buffalo for nothing."

She hurried over to her pack and returned with a gold watch.

Scarface's eyes widened with appreciation. He plucked the watch from Sally's hand and jammed it against his ear. He held his breath and listened for a moment, then a look of contempt filled his eyes.

Sally snatched the watch before he could throw it away in disgust. "Wind watch!" she said, demonstrating.

The Indian listened again. Now, he smiled broadly and motioned his companions forward. In a series of quick gestures, he deftly indicated he wanted each of his men to have a watch of his own.

Sally was heartsick yet knew she had no choice but to agree. "This'll clean me out!" she wailed.

"It's worth it, for God's sake."

Sally distributed the watches, repeating to each of the happy Indians, "Buffalo. You help us find buffalo."

To a man, they nodded enthusiastically, then they all remounted and Scarface yelled, "Buffalo!", drummed his moccasins into his pony's ribs and galloped off with his braves, who were yipping with joy.

"Wait!" Thomas cried, racing for the horses. "Wait for us!"

The Sioux rode on without a backward glance.

"I'll kill them if they think they can get away with my watches for nothing!" Sally screamed.

While Thomas saddled, she tossed everything into a saddle pack. No two people ever broke camp faster nor rode after seven Indians with more determination.

The Sioux, however, had no intention of trying to escape. Indeed, Sally and Thomas heard them whooping and calling back and forth to each other on the narrow mountain trail. And, when they rejoined them, the Indians imitated Sally and called, "Buffalo, buffalo!" They obviously thought the entire affair was hilarious.

Thomas was almost grateful for their company. Right now, Sally was not a fit person to ride the trail with alone.

On and on they traveled until long after dark, and then they camped without a fire. Thomas and Sally shared their jerky and biscuits, but the Indians did not seem at all pleased or grateful and finally one grunted, "Whiskey!"

"No whiskey. Buffalo," Thomas said.

There were a few nervous moments after that but, once the Indians were resigned to the fact that there was no whiskey, they became congenial again. They sat crosslegged around a campfire and sang and told what Thomas imagined were great stories, all the while gesticulating vigorously. He would have given almost anything to understand. Once again, he wished for Moose Mulligan's company instead of Sally's. Moose would have been able to learn how many buffalo they'd find and if there were any really prize bulls that Colonel Cody could use for his dwindling herd. Thomas resolved that, if everything went smoothly, he'd pay Moose something—if the old hunter hadn't believed that finding a herd of survivors was possible, I wouldn't be here now, Thomas reasoned to himself.

That night Sally moved her saddle and blankets next to

his, and though she smiled sweetly before lying down, Thomas wasn't deceived like the watchful Indians. Sally had no use for him; he guessed she preferred murderers like Rodney. Once they got away from any company, she'd be spreading her blankets across the fire just like always.

In the glow of firelight, he studied both Sally and the Indians. He examined the contrast of their features. The Sioux had angular facial lines, while Sally's were smooth and her face was heart-shaped. Her nose was short, a little dipped; theirs were slightly hooked. Thomas wondered how the Sioux judged a woman's looks. Did they think Sally as pretty as he did or did they, as he suspected, judge such things by an entirely different yardstick. Beauty was in the eye of the beholder, though a shapely woman of any race was a universal pleasure to watch.

Thomas thought he should stay awake, but the Indians were paying them no attention and his eyes grew heavy. Underneath the blankets he gripped his pistol, but it seemed to him that if these fellows had it in their minds to kill or rob them, they could do it anytime.

He closed his eyes and, just as he was drifting off, Sally jabbed him the ribs with her derringer—hard.

"Ouch!" he grunted.

He rolled over to confront her. "What'd you do that for, dammit!"

"If I've got to stay awake, then so do you," she hissed.

The Indians had stopped talking. Thomas could feel them watching and he guessed Sally did too. They hadn't understood the word "sister," and he knew that they were wondering if they'd make love under the blankets.

"They expect something from us," he said with devilish amusement.

"Then they're in for a hell of a big disappointment."

He grinned because she was now as wide awake as could be and looking plenty uncomfortable about the situation.

On an impulse, Thomas said, "Wouldn't hurt to give each other a little kiss just for appearances. Maybe then they'd quit staring."

Her face screwed up with distaste, but he could tell she was thinking it over pretty carefully.

"All right," she finally sighed. "But if you try to push your luck, I'll blow you a new belly button!"

Thomas felt the derringer poke into his stomach. He reached out and carefully drew her into his arms. This, he reminded himself for good measure, was an evil woman. A thief, a liar and possibly a murderess. But, when their lips touched, instead of hers being hard and cold as he'd expected, they were soft and warm. He pulled her closer and her body seemed to melt against his own. It was wonderful. Even with the sound of the Indians' approval, he couldn't believe how good she tasted and. . . .

He felt rather than heard the derringer being cocked.

Thomas froze. His lips withered against hers and when she tore her mouth away, she hissed, "Just ease back or so help me I'll pull the trigger."

Staring into her eyes, he had no doubt she meant it. He skidded away and the Indians hooted with derision. Thomas didn't care. He'd lost his head for a moment and almost his life.

He rolled over in hurt silence. Damn that girl anyway! There was no limit to her power over men. He glared at her back. All right, he vowed, I've tasted your sweet poison and you can damn sure bet I never will again.

Thomas awoke with a start. "Get up!" Sally whispered urgently. "We're breaking camp."

He shook his head groggily. "It's still dark," he protested. "Stars are out."

"The Sioux don't care."

Rolling out of his blankets, he quickly saddled his horse and followed the Indians out of camp, riding single file through the dense forest.

It wasn't even close to sunup as they climbed higher into the Big Horns. Thomas didn't try to guide his horse along the steep, boulder-strewn trail but instead let it pick its own footing. The air was nippy at this altitude and when they finally crested, they let their horses blow steam. Despite the circumstances and uncertainty, Thomas was awestruck by the beauty he saw reflected in the predawn light. Towering pines rose like dark city spires toward the fading stars, and the very highest peaks were mantled with snow and hung with magic luminescence in their proud, cold beauty.

The Sioux pushed on, now riding across big meadows, then into dark forests, then over rock-rimmed alpine valleys where snowdrifts lurked under rocks and trees even on the hottest days of the year. Thomas had no idea how far away the buffalo might yet be and was surprised that the Indians would stay up so late at night and then ride out long, long before dawn. Maybe they didn't need as much sleep as white people.

The Indians rode into another forest and Thomas immediately sensed a change in their mood. All conversation died and they now pushed their horses at a steady trot which devoured the hard miles.

Daylight tinged the eastern horizon; a thin gray line nudged insistently at the bowl of darkness. The snow's brilliance faded and newly silhouetted ridgelines emerged. They were climbing what had to be the final crest leading up into a valley. Thomas glanced sideways at Sally and both somehow knew they'd reached the place of the buffalo. Her face reflected weariness but also excitement.

The Indians reined a halt and spoke in low whispers. Then, they inspected their rifles and Scarface glanced at Thomas.

"Buffalo!" he cried, driving his horse forward.

"Don't kill them!" Thomas shouted. "Save buffalo!"

The Indians weren't listening. They slashed the barrels of their rifles across the rumps of their ponies and were off and racing over the hill.

"Let's go!" Sally cried.

Thomas needed no urging. When the first rifle shot boomed, his heart fell inside. "They're going to slaughter them!"

As they raced up and into the valley, the sun burst across the land, bathing it red, and there below them, scattering for their lives, were at least a hundred head of longhorn cattle.

Thomas could not believe his eyes. They'd misunderstood all along! And even as he and Sally swept down to halt the slaughter, he knew it was too late. The Sioux were flying off their horses, drawing knives and falling upon the carcasses like a pack of butchers.

"No!" Thomas yelled at Scarface. "These are *cattle*. Not buffalo. They are someone's cattle!"

Scarface didn't even look up. The cow he'd shot was dead but still twitching, and he was carving off part of her hindquarter.

"Look!" Sally cried, fighting to control her horse. "Riders!"

Thomas gaped. Not two miles away, small but somehow menacing, a body of horsemen was coming fast. He heard their rifles and though they were still out of range, it was chillingly obvious they were going to shoot first and ask questions later.

The Indians saw them, too. Scarface barked a warning. His own knife slashed even faster, and he was using it like an axe to hack off sections of hind quarter. He tied them together and managed to swing them over his pony's withers.

"We'd better get out of here quick," Sally yelled, "or we're in bad trouble!"

Thomas couldn't believe what was happening. It seemed impossible these Sioux could have misunderstood him so completely.

The last of Scarface's warriors loaded his kill and vanished into the forest. Now, their leader could follow but not until he waved in triumph and shouted, "You in heap big trouble, Thomas! Ride fast. Cattle rustlers catch, they hang you with thieving Injun!"

With that bit of advice, he galloped away.

"He knew!" Thomas shouted. "He understood everything!"

"Let's go!"

Thomas needed no further urging. Leading his packhorse, he saw an opening in the trees and darted for it with Sally crowding his heels and whipping their packhorse forward. They had about a mile lead on their pursuers and, with luck, they ought to be able to escape.

The game trail he followed vanished, and now Thomas was breaking a new path and paying dearly for it. Tree limbs smashed and whipped his body and deep thickets raked at his horse's legs, almost pulling the animal down. Somehow he held onto the packhorse, but he was so busy trying to avoid being knocked out of the saddle that he couldn't spare even a glance over his shoulder.

The gunfire grew distant and Thomas knew his horse was going to collapse if he didn't stop and let it rest. He figured they were safe for now but drew his rifle anyway. They'd run far enough. If need be, he and Sally could make a stand.

"Sally, we. . . ."

She wasn't there. Thomas grabbed her riderless horse and a mixture of cold dread and hot anger coursed through his veins. There was blood on the saddle.

He stared back through his path of broken limbs. There was nothing following him but silence.

"Sally," he whispered.

Thomas was going back. Sally was no damned good but she was his pardner and that said it all. Colonel Cody and Cyrus Rutherford could afford to wait a little longer for their damned old buffalo.

Wait long enough for him to find Sally.

CHAPTER 6

Thomas tried to remember how many riders had attacked them and decided it wasn't as many as he'd first thought. There hadn't been more than a half dozen, but they'd charged like the United States Cavalry. Scarface called them cattle rustlers and that made sense. This wasn't ranching country. With millions of acres of good prairie grass still free, no one would run cattle up in this mountain valley unless he was in hiding.

The more Thomas thought about it, the more he realized how difficult it was going to be finding out if Sally was still alive. If she wasn't, he'd head back to Laramie and alert a United States Marshall, then hope to return soon enough to catch these men and see them hang.

Now, as he retraced his path, Thomas was filled with misgivings. To be honest, he really hadn't done anything right for a long, long time; in fact, ever since his father had died. He'd started out by humiliating Franklin Pierce and being fired. Then, just when he'd gotten the chance of a lifetime, he'd let Sally and Rodney con him and steal all of Cyrus Rutherford's advance money. Not even a blow on the head had smartened him up because, in Cheyenne, he'd let his own pride stand in the way of good sense when he'd refused to team up with Pierce.

Well, he thought dejectedly, if I mess up this one, there won't be any more chances.

He came to the edge of the valley and carefully tied his horses back in the trees out of sight. When he returned to the clearing, he saw that the longhorns had been driven into the middle of the valley, just as far away from the trees as possible. Thomas watched the smoke of two branding fires and, even from a distance, he could smell the unpleasant odor of burnt hide and hair. The rustlers worked fast in two teams of three men each. Two on horseback would head and heel the cattle while the third man used a long, curved running iron to alter the original brand. It was fast, tough work and anyone could see these ropers were professionals while the brander was about half artist. All Thomas knew was what he'd read—a running iron could make a man as rich or as poor as a bookkeeper's penstrokes in a ledger book. But it could also get him in deep trouble.

Thomas had seen enough. The cattle weren't important —Sally was, and so he retreated back to his horses and began to work his way around to the distant cabin. If she was there, he wasn't going to hesitate a minute. He'd make a try for her at once.

It had taken Thomas longer to reach the cabin than he'd anticipated, and it was all he could do to sprint up to the rear of the little log building and up onto its roof before the cattle rustlers came riding in. He was out of breath and hadn't even had time to see if Sally was inside.

The riders turned their horses into a nearby pole corral and trudged wearily toward the cabin. Thomas listened to them argue about whose turn it was to cook and do dishes.

"Just you wait," one said. "In a couple of days, the girl will be fit to do it all and we can take it easy."

Thomas' mouth split into a wide grin. He'd learned what he'd hoped to learn. Being on the roof made sense now. He gritted his teeth with purpose, knowing there *had* to be a way.

"Hell," another said, "she'd better be fit by tomorrow."

"By tomorrow night, ya mean, don't ya! What we got to do is to draw straws for her!"

Thomas' knuckles whitened as crude laughter exploded up from below. He only hoped Sally wasn't conscious or she'd be filled with panic, half out of her mind with helpless fear.

And then he heard her voice. Weak, with just the slightest tremor, yet steady and assured as it carried out the door.

"You boys had better behave yourselves or when my husband comes back for me, he'll bring enough friends to hang your hides."

Good for you, Thomas thought, ignoring the taunts and wishing he could hug that girl because he was so proud. It made his throat tighten when he thought about how much courage it required to seem brave, thinking you were forsaken in a nest of cattle rustlers.

Just the thought of little Sally being at their cruel mercy was enough to drive him to action, and yet he knew he was a dead man if he didn't use his wits.

So he lay there all evening, listening to the men below, thinking maybe they'd say something that would help him figure a rescue plan. It grew dark and, at this altitude, when the sun went down so did the temperature. Once they closed the front door, he had to press his ear to the roof to listen and even then the words filtering up were indistinct and disjointed. What he did learn was that a cattle buyer was arriving from Laramie tomorrow afternoon to tell these men where they could deliver the stolen herd and the price they'd receive. Mostly, the talk was about the money they'd get and what kind of offer the new man would deliver and how they'd shoot the bastard like the last one if he made a poor offer.

Thomas was cold and stiff by the time the stars were blinking. He listened to a pack of coyotes howl up in the trees and began to worry lest they frighten his horses and cause them to break loose. That would really cap his uninterrupted string of failures. Afoot, he'd be in a hell of a mess.

Behind him, the tin stovepipe began to bang and up came a cloud of smoke and embers. Thomas thought hard about capping the pipe by stuffing his shirt down inside. This would cause an almost immediate evacuation but it seemed damned unlikely he'd be able to get the drop on all of them and, if the cabin burst into flames, both he and Sally might just be incinerated. Thomas decided he'd better return to the horses and try to think of something a little more intelligent.

It was late by the time he reached his hideout and, because he dared not light a fire, he chewed some more dried jerky and rolled up into his saddle blankets. Never had he felt so unequal to a challenge as he did to rescuing Sally. I can't fail, he thought, for either of our sakes.

Daybreak came early and found him in the saddle. During the night, he'd awakened with at least a semblance of a plan and, deep inside, he felt the beginning of hope.

He rode steadily all morning and, at noon, he found the trail leading up from Laramie that he'd known would exist. Excited now, he followed it at a brisk trot, putting as many miles between himself and the cattle rustlers' valley as possible. Two hours later, he came to a spot on the mountain trail where a horseman wouldn't have enough room to maneuver an escape. The trail fell off into a steep canyon on the downside and butted against a rock face on the other.

Thomas hid his horses and took a position behind a twisted pine tree. He dried his palms on his shirt and guessed he was as ready as he'd ever be.

The cattle buyer was late and pushing hard. Thomas heard the puffing of his horse and the clattering of its hooves a half mile away. He debated whether to use his rifle or his pistol and finally decided the rifle would seem more threatening. He'd kill this man if he had to in order to save Sally, but only as a last resort.

The rider came into view. He was tall and in his thirties, wearing a business suit with boots and a good Stetson. In the moment before Thomas moved, he had the impression of a very respectable citizen, much like a small town banker.

"Hold it!" Thomas yelled, jumping into the path of his horse.

The man checked his mount and then suddenly spurred forward. Thomas fired, then leapt sideways to avoid being trampled. The rifle was knocked spinning but he managed to grab the pommel and let the horse's forward momentum swing him up behind the saddle. The cattle buyer drove an elbow into his ribs and Thomas gasped for air and hung on tight. All right, he thought grimly, let's just see who can ride a bucking horse. And when the man tried to pull his gun, Thomas let his spurs tickle the horse's flanks.

The animal began to pitch like fury as it hopped along that ledge of trail. It didn't help matters at all when the buyer tore his pistol free and fired wildly into the air, his second bullet grazing his horse's shoulder. The beast went berserk with pain. Its owner lost both stirrups and, two jumps later, was tossed into the air. He yelped and then vanished over the ledge in a cloud of dust and a rattle of shale. It took Thomas better than a hundred yards and the best ride of his life to get the horse under control. And when he finally did, he realized how very close they'd both come to going over the edge in a fall neither might have survived.

"You're all right," he said quietly as he calmed the horse. The bullet wound across its right shoulder wasn't deep and he didn't think any muscles were torn. "Tomorrow you'll be limping pretty bad, but in a week you'll be ready to ride again."

He turned the horse around and carefully picked his way back along the trail. The footing was treacherous, loose, shifting rock that made him wonder how the animal had kept its feet.

The cattle buyer had tumbled about three hundred feet and would have gone much further if he hadn't slammed into a boulder and been knocked cold. It took some doing to reach him, but Thomas had no choice. An hour later he returned to the trail, out of breath but pleased with himself. He smoothed his mussed hair and tried on the cattle buyer's Stetson. It was a size too big, just like the coat, but the pants and sleeves were fine.

Thomas peered back over the ledge. The man was still wearing his underclothes and his boots, but that was all. Thomas gave in to sympathy and pitched his own torn shirt and pants down the mountainside.

"By the time you hike back to Laramie," he said, "those ought to fit you about right."

It was almost dusk and the light was fading as he crossed the valley, skirting the longhorns on his way to the log cabin. Over and over, Thomas kept reminding himself of the conversation he'd overheard. They'd said "a cattle buyer." That implied a stranger. If he'd figured wrong, he was as good as dead in the next minute and a half, but the guns in his coat pockets said he wouldn't go alone.

"You can stop right there, mister."

Thomas reined up. He smiled, though it must have looked like a death grin.

"Pretty good-looking bunch of cattle you got this time," he said easily. "Price for quality beef is up right now."

"So we've heard." The man doing the talking was older than the others. He was short and bandylegged, an ornery looking cuss who now approached with the hint of a swagger. "You can call me Alex," he said by way of introduction. With that, formalities were over. "How much for the herd?"

"Can't say yet."

"Sure you can."

He shook his head. "Light is too poor this time of day. I'll have to wait until tomorrow to give you a price. Tell you what, though. Those brands you changed are as good as any I've ever seen."

This pleased the stout little man whom Thomas remembered had been one of those using a running iron. "I'm the best. Better even than Dudley Foster."

Thomas considered that for a minute, then delivered what amounted to a verdict. "Your work makes Dudley's look sick."

"Well . . . well, thank ya kindly! I wouldn't go that far, but true is true. Step on down and come inside. We got a new cook I think you'll like the looks of, young fella."

The way he said it brought a ripple of laughter from the others, the kind of laughter that came up from the belly— or lower. Thomas was grateful for the poor light because he flushed with anger.

He dismounted and someone led his horse away. They

would check the saddlebags, of course, and they'd find the letter Thomas had transferred from the cattle buyer's pocket; it instructed him to pay up to thirty-eight dollars a head. Delivery date and destination had been omitted. In fact, there were no names on the letter at all, and that worried him considerably. If names were brought up in conversation, he was going to have to bluff and hope for the best.

But as he entered the cabin, those things were secondary and the moment he saw Sally, all his misgivings and worries evaporated.

She was lying on a bunk with her back to him. Her leg was bandaged, but he could see no other signs of injury. Thomas almost took an involuntary step toward her but caught himself, knowing any show of recognition would put their lives in even greater jeopardy. He prayed that his unexpected arrival wouldn't be such a shock that she'd re-act impulsively and call out his name. Try as he might, Thomas could think of no way to announce his presence gently without raising suspicions.

"Hey, wake up, girl. We got us a visitor. Get up and cook. You can sleep later."

"Never mind her," he said loudly. "Probably can't cook worth a damn anyway. Never met a pretty girl who could."

She'd been facing the wall on a lower bunk and now she rolled over quickly. Even in poor light, he could see her eyes widen and a cry of joy forming in her throat.

"Who is she?" Thomas barked sharply.

Sally clamped her mouth shut.

"Damned if she'll say. We caught her and some Indians butchering our beef. They all got away, 'cept her. That's why we want to leave here tomorrow for sure and get rid of those cattle."

"Don't blame you." Thomas couldn't keep his eyes off Sally. He'd never seen a girl look so good in such a bad situation.

Alex looked from one of them to the other. "As you can plainly see, the girl is mighty pretty."

"Sure is. What are you going to do with her?"

"We haven't decided yet." Alex looked away, mouth crimped and small. "That's our worry."

It didn't sound very promising. Sally could identify them as cattle thieves. Because of that, she was dangerous.

Sally did cook, but she was limping badly. It was hard not to try to help her, but there wasn't any choice. Alex and his men uncorked the whiskey, then began to talk cattle prices. They insisted that their herd of stolen longhorns were top-grade cattle and, therefore, worth at least forty-five dollars a head. Thomas argued more with frowns and scowls than words. He figured they'd be suspicious if he gave in too easily, so he offered thirty-five dollars.

"Have all you want of these steaks," Alex said. "God-damn thievin' Indians cost us plenty. Might as well eat what we can before it spoils."

The beef was tough but tasty. Sally gave Thomas the biggest steak of all and he ate like a famished wolf. The whiskey bottles kept going around but he drank almost nothing. If these men wanted to leave in the morning, then he and Sally were getting away tonight.

It was hard to keep track of the conversation, worry about Sally hopping around serving these men and think of some way out of this fix all at the same time. Thomas hoped the rustlers got drunk and then escape would be easy after they fell asleep. And if. . . .

"Stop it!" Sally suddenly snapped at a big man who

hadn't said a word yet who'd never taken his eyes from her. "Leave me alone!"

He grabbed her wrist, twisted it hard and brought her white-faced to her knees.

Thomas knocked over his chair. "Let go of her!"

"Best not tell Ned how to behave," Alex advised softly. "He'll break you like a matchstick."

"I said, let go of her!"

This time, he did. Ned flung her arm away, then pivoted on the balls of his feet. When he stood up, Thomas saw that he was well over six feet tall and weighed at least two hundred pounds. He didn't exactly smile as he beat his fists into his palms, but he looked plenty excited.

"You want trouble, sonny?"

Thomas swallowed drily. No matter what he said, he was going to get trouble and it would probably be a whole lot more than he could handle.

"I want you to leave the girl alone," he said, wondering how in the world he might sidestep this without taking a beating.

Alex tried to placate the brute. "Ned, why don't you forget it. He didn't mean anything."

Ned came up to jab a thick forefinger into Thomas' chest. "You ready to shut up?"

Thomas smiled, raised both hands in a gesture of innocence, then punched him right in his grinning mouth as hard as he'd ever hit any man.

Ned rocked back on his heels, his eyes momentarily mirroring pain and disbelief. Then he purposefully spit out a tooth and snarled, "Now you done it." As the others hurriedly moved out of the way, Ned came in swinging.

He was slow and an easy target. Thomas ducked a windmill right and sank a fist into the man's stomach, which felt like a board fence. Ned reared back and landed a haymaker that numbed Thomas' shoulder and almost paralyzed his entire left arm. When Ned grabbed him by the shirt, Thomas had a moment of wild panic. He struggled, then punched Ned in the throat. The man's face drained and his tongue spilled out as he fought for breath.

Thomas used the moment to great advantage. His fists beat a tattoo against Ned's face and every blow knocked him back a step until he sat down on the iron stove. He bellowed like a branded bull and jumped up cursing and swinging.

A blow knocked Thomas into the wall, but he ducked an overhand right and heard Ned screech with a broken hand. Thomas slipped around him and drove two hard punches into his kidneys, then planted his feet and swung so hard his feet left the ground. His fist exploded against Ned's jaw and he staggered.

Someone splashed water into Ned's face and yelled, "Come on, Ned, kill the sonofabitch!"

Thomas waited because they made him give Ned time to recover.

"Now, get him!"

Ned wanted to. Face battered and swelling, lips broken, knuckles broken too, he looked more determined than ever and that just scared the hell out of Thomas. He'd never seen anyone take so much punishment and come back for more. The man seemed invincible and Thomas had serious doubts if he had enough remaining strength to stop him.

Sally picked up a frying pan but someone noticed and batted it away, then knocked her roughly aside.

Ned lunged and Thomas darted under his outstretched hands. When the man whirled around, Thomas hit him twice—once with each fist in both of his eyes.

Blinded by tears, Ned groped forward and Thomas hit him three more licks before the big man collapsed on the floor.

"Stay down," Thomas said quietly. "It's finished."

But it wasn't. Like a bad dream you couldn't escape, Ned was crawling back to his feet. He had a bottle of whiskey in his fist and gulped it, letting it spill down his bloody shirtfront. Thomas watched the life pouring back into the man, saw those swelling eyes grow mean and bright once more. What do I have to do to beat him, he asked, trying not to panic.

In a desperate situation like this, Thomas' father would have yelled at him to grab a club but Thomas knew he'd never be allowed to use it.

"I'm going to break you in half," Ned gasped. "Then I'm going to pleasure the girl."

Thomas sprang at him, bashed him twice and then jumped back as a roundhouse right moved air and sent Ned off balance. Again, Thomas used the opportunity and his fists drove into Ned's ribs. The man groaned and, just when Thomas thought he could finish it, someone jerked the bedroll he'd stepped on right out from under his feet. He fell hard and Ned lit on top of him like a mountain. Thomas rolled his head sideways but Ned sledgehammered him with a punch that deadened his face and made his head whirl. The man grabbed him by the hair and cocked back his fist for the blow that would knock him senseless.

Thomas looked up into that cruel, battered face and knew that the man was going to beat him to death. He heard Sally yelling his name and knew she too was fighting.

Ned arched his powerful back and Thomas did the only thing he could do and that was to kick his legs up and spur Ned with both feet across the neck. The spurs weren't

sharp like the Spaniards used, but they were meant for
raking horsehide and Ned's throat must have seemed like
butter in comparison.

Thomas dug them in hard and Ned roared as Thomas
flipped him over backward. The big man's skull slammed
on the floor and he finally lay stunned and beaten.

Thomas rolled up on one elbow and then Sally was help-
ing him to his feet, washing his face with cold water and,
without a word, telling him with her eyes how she felt
about him now.

They carried Ned outside and most of them stayed with
him, drinking in their anger and disappointment over the
outcome.

Dinner was forgotten.

Alex was watching him and Sally, and there was a
strange look on his face that made Thomas uneasy. Sally
must have noticed it too, because she moved off by herself.

"Let's go outside. I want to talk to you alone."

"Sure," Thomas said, watching Alex dig another bottle
of whiskey out of his bag. The man was already half drunk.
It looked as if it was going to be a long night.

None of the others said a word to them as they drifted
on out to the corral. Thomas didn't even see Ned, though
he could hear him cursing in the darkness somewhere
nearby.

The horses moved away from them and snorted, ears up
and heads alert. Thomas thought of his own horses tied off
in the forest waiting.

Alex shook his head in wonder. "I saw you do it—we all
did—but I still can't believe you whipped Ned. Soon as
he's able to, he'll want to fight you again."

"He will?"

"Sure. We all know you'd never beat him again."

"I believe you're right," Thomas said, massaging his battered knuckles.

"Tell me something. What is it between you and that girl? You know her from someplace?"

Thomas averted his face for an instant. "Naw, it's just that sometimes you see a girl and. . . ."

"Forget it. I feel that way even about fat and ugly ones." Alex chuckled. "But *this* girl, well, I just admire her spunk. Be a shame to kill her."

"Then don't."

"Have to. She could identify you now, same as us."

"But she wouldn't."

"Not you, maybe. You just played hero. But what about Ned? You think she'd hesitate to put a rope around his neck?"

"Why are you telling me this, Alex?"

He drank until he choked and coughed, then had to clear his throat to speak. His voice sounded raw as a rope burn. "I'm no woman killer. It's eating me up inside. Thought you might have an answer."

So, Thomas thought, here is either an opportunity or a trap. Which is it?

"You want *me* to kill her?"

"I don't think you could, any more than me."

"You're right about that."

"Ned will do it if I let him. He'll take her out in the woods and use her first. Then he'll do it."

"I'd kill him first," Thomas said through clenched teeth.

Alex chewed on that for a minute in silence while Thomas held his breath, wondering what the man was thinking. When Alex finally did start talking again, it had nothing to do with Sally.

"Tell you something I wouldn't admit to the others. I

want to quit this business before I get hung. I've never had any luck and cattle rustling will get an unlucky man hung."

"So, quit now."

"Uh-uh. Not until this job is over. I just need one good payday. One good one for all the times I've been broke and hungry. Hell, I've chased every gold strike from California to Colorado, from Mexico to Alaska. Always too late. Tried earning a living hunting buffalo but I was ten years too late again. We almost wiped them off the map."

"What do you mean, almost?"

"Almost. That's what I mean." He scowled. "I'll be honest with you. I'm worried about getting caught with this herd. The Wyoming Stock Growers' Association has hired a bunch of range detectives who shoot first and ask questions later. They got a few of them that make Ned look like a choirboy. Last year, I tried to go honest and get started with my own herd. Then they passed that damned Maverick Law saying that any unbranded calf without a mother to show who it belongs to is the Association's. That's cattle rustling, same as what I'm doing, only it's legal."

He was clearly outraged. He rolled a smoke and continued. "Whoever said the rich get richer and the poor get poorer had it figured out right. You know whose longhorns those are?"

"No."

"They belong to a very rich English nobleman who came out this spring and bragged about how the Maverick Law would hang a dozen rustlers before this year was over. He said only the wealthy classes should own land because the rest of us are too ignorant to handle it properly. Can you believe that!"

"I've known some Englishmen. A few still think there ought to be a feudal system, but not many."

"Oh, we'll feud, all right. I'd steal him blind, only I can see that the day of reckoning is coming up fast. Little man is being pushed off the range. He drove away the Indian and their buffalo and now that he's done the dirty work, he's not welcome to own land in Wyoming."

"You said there were some wild buffalo still out there. I'd like to know where."

Alex winked. "Oh no, you don't. That's a secret."

"But why?"

" 'Cause I like 'em, that's why. Big old dumb sumbitches. Leave 'em in peace."

"Forget it," Thomas said impatiently. Then, to needle Alex gently, "Anyhow, I don't believe they exist free anymore."

"Believe what you want to. I don't give a damn. Besides, what are we talking about buffalo for? We got a girl in that cabin to decide about."

He spun around and almost lost his balance. Thomas hadn't realized how drunk Alex was until now. His eyes wouldn't focus and he was swaying on his feet so badly he had to grip a rail to steady himself.

"Now," he said, squeezing one eye shut to keep from seeing double. "Thing is, are *you* gonna kill her for me quick or save her and get her outa this territory so she won't tell the Association about us?"

Thomas realized then that this wasn't some carefully thought out trap. Alex, despite everything, was a good man and he desperately wanted to save Sally's life. "I'll take her out of here," he promised. "You've my word she won't go to the authorities. Why don't you come with us?"

"Can't. Too late."

"No, it's not."

But Alex's mind was made up. "You tell me where to

deliver the cattle and give me a letter authorizing payment for forty dollars a head. Do that, and ride out tonight while we're asleep."

"You'd trust me?"

"Have to or Ned rapes the girl. Terrible, what he'd do. Besides, the girl likes you. I can tell. When I was your age, I had a girl like that for awhile. Lost her, though. Ran off with the gold fever. Came back, she'd married a farmer. Only girl ever looked at me that way."

Thomas felt awful, but he said what he had to say. "Forty dollars then."

"Good. Doan' forgit the letter tellin' us where to take 'em. Be jest in time for my sixty-third birthday."

"Come on," Thomas said, "let's get you to bed."

Thomas scribbled a note that read: *Alex, you have run out of luck in Wyoming Territory. Association could be on its way. Run for California!*

He emptied his pockets of his own money and what he'd taken from the real cattle buyer. All together, it added up to over a hundred dollars. Enough to ride the train first class to Sacramento and still have plenty left to fall back on until he got an honest job. Thomas regretted that he hadn't been able to confess to Alex that he wasn't really a cattle buyer. He also regretted the man hadn't told him where those buffalo yet roamed. But Alex believed they were still out there and so did Moose Mulligan. Two old-timers maybe letting nostalgia work their mouths. The old ones did that sometimes when they looked back on what seemed like better days. Their wishes came tumbling out and you could look them in the eye and, when you did, you knew better than to tell them the past was gone, that every-thing they remembered—the girls, the good horses and dogs and friends, the fun and the love—it was all tied up in an empty package called yesterday. And any fool who tried to pull the old ones back into today ought to be ashamed. If the old wanted to live in the past, then let them do it because the past was free.

Sally tugged on his arm. Gun in hand, Thomas, together with the girl, crept outside and drank in the clean, crisp night air.

"Thank you!" she whispered, throwing her arms around his neck and hugging him with all her strength.

Thomas laughed quietly and then they were saddling a pair of horses and roping the others together. He lowered the corral gate and they trotted away across the moonlit valley. Longhorn cattle smelling of burned hide paid them no attention. He wondered what would become of these longhorns now. Thomas hoped that Alex, at least, would be wise enough to take his found money and hike to the nearest train depot and buy a westbound ticket.

A half hour later, they came to the two horses he'd left with their pack and provisions.

"Thomas, you have amazed me and I must say I'm ashamed of all the things I thought about you before tonight. I figured you'd be on a train for Boston first chance."

"Well, I'm not. I'm going after buffalo. You still want to go along?"

"Nothing could stop me," she told him happily. "Especially now that we got us seven extra horses to trade to the Indians. Next to gold watches, there's not a thing in this world an Indian likes better!"

Thomas opened his mouth, then clamped it shut. Some things and some people just defy description.

CHAPTER 7

From that day on, Sally changed toward him in a way Thomas didn't attempt to understand. Sometimes, he caught her watching him and then her cheeks would color almost as if . . . as if she were in love.

But then there were other times when she treated him like a stranger and her eyes grew distant. Thomas was certain she was remembering Rodney Laird that last time as he had looked on the gallows. His expression was haunting her. Thomas was sure it was and yet he knew she would never speak of it to anyone. Rodney was a ghost that floated between them. He worried about Sally when he saw that stricken look in her eyes. A hundred times, he almost told her to forget the man—he'd gotten what he'd deserved and now she was free, if she'd only let go of his memory. She could have her pick now, marry and start a family of her own. But Sally never talked about such things. She was bright and well-versed in world affairs and would talk for hours about politics, religion, the weather, the world and buffalo. She would not, however, talk about herself.

Anyway, she was in good spirits most of the time and fun to be with, if you knew the rules and abided by them. Thomas never again came around at night to her side of the campfire, where she fell asleep almost as soon as she closed her eyes.

As for himself, he liked to tend the fire and allow his mind to drift. Usually, he thought about Alice, though he was disturbed to learn that it was sometimes hard to recall her face precisely or just how her laughter sounded. This angered him, for it hadn't been that long since he'd last seen her and wanted to tell her of his love and his dream to find the buffalo and make his fortune. And while the image of her face and the sound of her laughter had faded, he was convinced now more than ever that he *would* find buffalo and win the prize money.

Perhaps his confidence was not justified, but everyone out West was banking on a dream. Everyone thought big— a gold strike, a cattle ranch, a freight line or even a saloon, a business venture almost certain to succeed. Out here, men won and lost fortunes almost routinely. They would gamble a lifetime's earnings on the turn of a card, a roll of the dice or the nose of a fast horse.

When he'd expressed his amazement at the willingness of Westerners to take risks, Sally had explained it by saying, "They believe money is to be spent, not hoarded; fortunes to be gambled, not left to mildew in some vault. To build this country, we have to work hard and so does our money. If we don't use it, no towns, schools, roads or ranches would be built. It's the *game* that counts, Thomas, not just the final score."

Thomas thought about that quite a bit, and he wasn't so sure it wasn't true. According to the standards of most men, the score was the wealth they'd managed to accumulate. But you could only spend so much money in a day, or have so much fun, and a lot of people derived more pleasure from catching a fish, riding a horse or hearing a good story than anything else. Those things were almost free. Thomas had been around Cyrus Rutherford and his wealthy friends enough to know they weren't any happier in their day-to-day living than most people who liked what they did.

And speaking of day to day, it occurred to him one crisp morning when he found ice along a stream, that it was autumn and they'd ridden the Big Horn Mountains clear into Montana Territory. Before him, the high northern plains unfolded into the distance like a rumpled blanket. As far as the eye could see, there were only mountains, grass and sky.

Thomas consulted his map. "If we keep riding north along the Big Horn River, we'll come to the Yellowstone River."

"Then what do we do?"

He shrugged. "Looks like good buffalo country all around to me. But I was told our best chance would be to follow the Yellowstone a while."

"A while?" Sally's eyebrows arched. "Does that mean a week, or a month? A hundred miles or a thousand? Where are we?"

There was just enough concern in her voice to worry Thomas. "We'll find a settlement, maybe even a fort, and with seven horses to trade, we'll be fine."

Sally didn't look very convinced and yet she was too proud or stubborn to argue. She didn't remind Thomas that they were out of almost everything, either. He'd shot an antelope a week before, but what remained of it had spoiled.

Thomas was worried, too, but not about hunger. Twice that morning, he'd seen Indians on the horizon and he hoped they were friendly. As the day progressed, the feeling that they were being watched grew stronger and, by midafternoon, he saw them approaching.

There were perhaps a half dozen men, and Thomas saw that two of them had antelope draped across their horses' withers. Each warrior had a rifle and yet Thomas did not feel they were in any particular danger. This was Crow Indian country and the Crow had usually been friendly to the whites. Still, it was the "usually" that could get you scalped.

Thomas took a deep breath. "Well, Sally, I'll let you do the talking like before. I'm sure you can parlay in their own language."

"Quiet," she said cryptically. "Just smile and hold your hand up in a gesture of friendship."

The Indians reined up about twenty yards from them and sat watching and waiting.

"Friends," Sally said.

The Crow considered that for several minutes. Flies buzzed, horses stomped and Thomas felt a trickle of sweat river down his backbone even though the day was cool. He prayed these men understood English and, a moment later, his prayers were answered.

"Where you from?" a handsome young warrior dressed in half an army uniform asked.

"From Cheyenne." Thomas gestured back toward the horses. "We come to trade for food, supplies and . . . buffalo."

The warrior's expression remained unchanged, but he answered with bitterness. "Buffalo gone. Crow have nothing to trade. Talk with Winfield."

"Who's he?"

"Indian agent. Come. We show." Then, abruptly, the Indians rode off without waiting or apparently even expecting an answer.

Thomas and Sally exchanged questioning glances.

"I think we'd better follow them," Sally said.

Thomas was hungry and there were big thunderheads piling up to the north. A cool wind sprang up and the grass began to flatten before it. He'd been out here long enough to know this land was in for a cold drenching, and that helped to decide the issue.

"Let's go," he said, pushing his horse into a trot and dragging their string of pack animals along behind them.

They were soaked through and shivering, but just ahead lay the Crow village. Thomas saw perhaps fifty gray tepees staked down in a low cluster of hills. Overhead, lightning flashed and thunder rolled, then crashed. Indian ponies stood tied forlornly beside their owners' tepees, their tails whipped down between their legs. Children dashed through the encampment and then disappeared. Dogs barked more out of habit than conviction and then slunk off to wait out the storm.

To the west of the village, Thomas could see a huge field of corn stubble and beyond it a long ditch that zigzagged up into the hills. The ditch was already filled with rainwater and its banks were broken down in so many places that brown, muddy water was spilling out down the hill, bleeding through the green grass. The field itself appeared sodden and defeated. It looked like a failure.

They stopped in front of a tepee and one of their escort called out, "Jones!" Almost immediately, the door flap was thrown back to reveal a thin white man who wore glasses and a full beard. He looked gentle, almost benign.

"Come inside," he said, "before you both catch pneumonia. My friends will take care of your horses and outfits. You've nothing to worry about."

Thomas hesitated. If they lost. . . .

"Come on!" Sally urged, almost falling out of the saddle.

Thomas had no choice but to trust this man and follow. Besides, to do otherwise would have been insulting.

The tepee was warm and dry. A fire danced happily in a circle of rocks and, beyond it, a pretty young Indian woman was nursing an infant. "Welcome," she said, "our home is yours."

Sally smiled gratefully. They were both dripping puddles on the earth floor, but no one seemed to notice.

"Here," the man said, bringing up two warm buffalo robes. "Take off your wet clothes and wrap yourselves in these. You'll be dry and warm in no time."

Sally's smile evaporated. She glanced nervously at Thomas, then at her host. "If you don't mind, we'll just huddle beside the fire and let it dry us."

"Aren't you married?" the man asked, looking from one to the other of them with deep concern. "If not, I will marry you according to the laws of God and my church."

"Well, of. . . ." Sally clamped her mouth shut and gazed at a large cross dangling from one of the poles. "Well, no, Reverend," she whispered, "we are not."

"Then you shall be! For to live together without the sanctity of holy marriage is to live in sin. My wife, Tame Doe, will help prepare you for the ceremony."

"No," Thomas said quickly, "you don't understand. We aren't living together. We're just *traveling* together."

"Traveling together?" He frowned with grave disapproval.

"Yes," Sally said. "We are business partners."

"What kind of business?" the Reverend asked skeptically.

Thomas quickly explained.

The Reverend protested, "There are no buffalo in these parts. It's been at least five years since the last hunt. I

wasn't here then but I'm told the Crow found only two—
an old, old bull and a cow that some whites had shot for
sport and left to die. The tribe mourned for weeks. Their
way of life was over. The next winter was the first time they
experienced starvation. To the Plains Indian, the buffalo
was life."

The flap to the tepee opened a crack and a piece of meat
no larger than a doubled up fist was extended. The Indian
spoke a few quick words, then disappeared. The Reverend
gave the modest portion to his wife, who took it almost
reverently and then began to cut it into thin slices and
drape them over green willow sticks she had placed across
the rock ring. To this was added a beaten pot holding about
an inch of water. Tame Doe waited until the water boiled
and then took an almost empty leather pouch and sprinkled
in cornmeal, stirring it to prevent burning. Thomas' mouth
watered with anticipation and yet he could not help but
wonder how so little could satisfy the four of them.

Maybe Sally was thinking along these same lines because
she smiled at the Indian woman and said, "It smells deli-
cious. We've just eaten a short time ago so we're not hungry. Are we, Tom?"

"No," he gulped, patting the skin stretched over his
belly like a hollow drum. "Sure aren't."

"You're both guilty of breaking the sixth of God's com-
mandments," Jones said, "but the Lord will understand
that your intentions are worthy of praise. What we have,
we share. No one will starve. Very soon, we'll receive our
monthly allotment."

"Allotment?" Thomas hadn't heard the term used before.

"Yes. That's what the Bureau calls them. What they
really are is charity. The Indians are given just enough to

survive but no more. Each month, we get weeviled flour, sugar, beans, cornmeal and whatever meat the army has deemed unfit for consumption."

The way he said it left no doubt as to his anger. But if there wasn't enough food being allocated to the Crow, as there apparently wasn't, then it seemed to him that the proper authorities ought to be made accountable.

"Can't something be done?"

"We're trying. The problem is that the United States Army is in charge of the reservations and they are Indian haters. Career officers are promoted on the basis of their success in exterminating and capturing the Indian. Do you really think they want the Indian people healthy and well fed?"

The question called for no response. Thomas and Sally ate the thin strips of antelope meat but not the cornmeal gruel, which Tame Doe fed to her baby, saving what remained.

Thomas listened while the Reverend talked about the sad plight of the Indian, especially the young men who had to steal away at night like fugitives in their own land to hunt off the reservation. If caught, they would be handcuffed and herded back like criminals. They might also be shot by whites, and there'd be no questions asked.

"You see," the Reverend explained, "the Indian boy cannot be considered a man until he has proven himself in battle and as a hunter or horse catcher. But according to the whites, all of these things must end. So what is a young man to do?"

"I saw the cornfields," Sally interrupted. "Maybe that is the answer."

Reverend Jones laughed with a brittle sound. "This isn't cropland and these aren't farming people. Still, they tried.

God knows, they tried. Perhaps you saw the miles of irrigation ditches, the fallow fields. Because our Indian agent could spare only three shovels, we dug with our fingers, with sticks and knives. The first year, the corn seed was bad and failed to germinate. The second year was different, the corn grew right up until we began to harvest hulls full of worms. This year, it was locusts and an early frost. There won't be a next year."

"I wish there was some way we could help."

"There isn't. Only God could do something, and the Indians have lost whatever faith I might have given them."

"Have *you?*" Sally asked quietly.

The Reverend stared into the fire, a man obviously being tested to the depths of his soul. It was only when his baby began to cry that he looked up and extended his hands to Tame Doe.

"This," he said fervently, as he held the baby up and it stared with big brown eyes at them, "is the thing that keeps me whole. I am like a baby in the hands of God. My eyes do not yet focus and I cannot think—only feel pain. But if I can survive and grow, if the Indian can last, God will show him His plan."

He held the baby until it stopped crying and then he said, "In a few days, we go to Winfield, our agent. If you come, he may not try to cheat us this time. Will you stay until then?"

Both Thomas and Sally nodded, knowing they'd stay as long as was necessary.

The meat was gone and so was the cornmeal. It was raining a cold, penetrating drizzle. Tame Doe and all the women except Sally remained in their tepees while the men hitched up old carts and wagons for the twenty-mile journey. If there had been any food left to share in the village, everyone would have gone and camped overnight. With full stomachs, there would have been dancing and singing and the children would have laughed and played games.

But now, as they plodded down a puddled track across the Montana prairie, everyone knew they'd be coming back today, no matter how late, in order to feed the women and children.

The wagons and carts kept bogging down in the low places, and all of Thomas and Sally's horses were put into harness before midday. By the time they finally approached the agent's post, they were all mud-covered and staggering.

A body of soldiers in knee-length rain slickers emerged to stand beside canvas-covered provision wagons, and Thomas noticed they were armed with repeating rifles. It made him wonder if there'd ever been a food riot.

The Reverend Jones had explained that these distributions took place once a week because the Indian agent insisted the Crow live and be fed in separate groups.

The Indians stood in the rain several minutes before the agent, a fat, cigar-chewing man with an air of authority that made the hackles rise, squinted at Thomas and Sally, then said, "Who are they?"

"Guests," the Reverend replied, looking very pleased with things.

"They reporters?"

"Do they look like reporters?"

Winfield peered at them and massaged his red jowls. "No," he said finally. "Too dirty. Let's get this over with."

He pulled out a wadded notebook and stump of pencil. "Anybody die this past month?" he asked, almost hopefully.

"Sorry to disappoint you, Mr. Winfield," the Reverend said with contempt.

"Then you get food enough for two hundred and six."

"Two hundred and seven. Spotted Horse's wife blessed him with a son."

Thomas noticed that the Indian agent wasn't pleased as he scribbled in the new figure.

"Ain't fair the government has to pay the same for a damned papoose as a full-growed buck." He twisted around and signaled to the waiting detail of soldiers, who immediately began to untie the canvas coverings. "You and the Indians can reload in your own wagons, seeing as how you're already soaked."

"What kind of a man are you!" Thomas exploded. "These people have come twenty miles on empty bellies. They are tired and hungry."

"Who the hell asked you?" the Indian agent bellowed. "This is a government Indian reservation and I'm in charge."

"Then do your job!"

"Or we will write the New York *Daily* about it," Sally added vengefully. "It's time the people back East learned the truth about the cheating going on."

Winfield's cheeks puffed out and he looked ready to explode but, when he spoke, you could tell that Sally had him half convinced she really was a journalist.

"Lady," he gasped, "maybe you and him ought to come inside out of the rain. I'm sure we can be reasonable about this."

"Not on your life, buster. I just want to see these Indians get what they have coming so we can leave. There are hungry women and children waiting for us."

Winfield gave the order and the soldiers jumped into

action as the Reverend and several Indians stood beside
their own wagons and inspected the sacks and barrels of
beans, flour, corn and potatoes.

Every few minutes, one of them would turn out to be
weevil-ridden or spoiled and the Reverend would order it to
be unloaded. This always caused a bitter argument but the
Reverend, to Thomas' amazement, stood his ground. The
man just would not be intimidated.

It took nearly an hour to load the wagons and, by then,
they were all shivering with the cold. The Reverend had
some kind of tally sheet, and he and two of the tribal elders
were talking in Crow. It didn't require a translator to see
the tally wasn't adding up.

"What's wrong now?" the agent groused.

"You know very well we are short on fish and salt pork.
And I still haven't seen the six dozen wool blankets we
need for winter."

"Two dozen. That's all I promised."

"Six." The Reverend's voice was chipped ice. "The
nights are growing cold. The surface of the water is frozen
every morning. Our blankets are worn thin."

"Then have 'em ask their medicine man to pray for a
warm winter."

The Reverend maintained his composure, though how
Thomas couldn't imagine.

"I'll expect the blankets and those other items to be here
when we return the day after tomorrow, Mr. Winfield."

He turned then and left the Indian agent standing in the
rain, hating him. Minutes later, they were rolling back
across the prairie.

"What a crook!" Sally grated between her chattering
teeth. "I'll bet anything he's selling what belongs to these
Indians and filling his own pockets."

"It's almost expected," the Reverend answered. "The government pays them almost nothing and yet they come out here broke and leave quite wealthy. They sell their souls."

"Is it like this everywhere?"

"I can't be certain, but probably. The white man's treatment of the Indians will prove to be a dirty stain on the pages of American history. Mark my words."

Thomas figured that was close enough to the truth of the matter. The whole situation was as depressing as the weather. Night fell like a gray, sodden blanket and they pushed on in weary silence. With the clouds covering both moon and stars, it was pitch black and there was a steady, cutting wind from the northeast. Rarely had Thomas been so cold and miserable. He couldn't imagine where they were or even how long they had ridden.

Sometime past midnight, though, it stopped raining and the clouds opened up to show the moon sailing across a brilliant, diamond-studded sky. And just about the time Thomas was beginning to recognize a few landmarks, Sally suddenly keeled over and fell out of the saddle.

He was at her side in an instant. Perhaps it was the moonlight, but her face was the sickly color of a wax candle and it scared him when he touched her cheeks and felt how warm they were.

"She's burning up with a fever!"

The Reverend wasted no time making a place for her in one of the wagons. "Get in beside her in case she becomes delirious. When we reach the village, I'll have Tame Doe brew some medicinal herbs."

Thomas nodded. He gently placed Sally between the sacks and then removed his coat and climbed under it, pulling her close. He wondered how long she'd been sick and why she hadn't given them any warning. Except for her one outburst at the Indian agent, she'd been unusually quiet this day, but he'd thought she was just tired.

"Dammit," he whispered. "One of these days, you're going to have to start letting someone help you once in awhile."

She didn't answer, but he realized then that she was awake because her arms squeezed him tightly.

After a rain, the sun glistens on prairie grass and the world seems to focus almost too sharply. Thomas noted how the sky and the hills melded into the distance and he listened as Crow children burst outside to bathe in the sunshine.

He felt good, and even Sally was much better. Tame Doe was giving her regular doses of some vile-tasting concoction that worked like magic in restoring her health and color.

"She's going to be fine after a couple of days rest," the Reverend said. "She's a strong woman."

"Too strong for her own good."

"You say that with pride and," he added knowingly, "with love."

There was enough truth in the observation to make a strong denial useless. "I admire her," Thomas said. "But I'm in love with a girl named Alice Rutherford."

"And she loves you?"

"Not yet—but she will."

"How do you know?"

Thomas frowned. "Maybe I don't know for sure," he admitted. "But I hope to win her by proving I can make something of myself."

"You mean by earning money from the buffalo?"

"Yes."

"Thomas, the Bible is filled with examples of how money confuses and stands in the way of real love."

"Money can buy respect and out of respect grows love," he argued.

"God teaches us to love our fellow man, even one like Mr. Winfield. But we certainly don't have to respect him. Besides, I'm sure that young lady cares deeply for you."

Thomas almost told him about the *real* Sally. But he didn't. A man of God like him might never recover from the shock and probably wouldn't believe him anyway. Sally, of course, had put on her public mask, the one that could blind anyone to her true nature.

The Reverend must have taken his silence for acceptance. "I think you should marry that girl."

"I'll give it serious thought if I ever change my mind about Miss Alice," he said, "but right now, all I care about is finding some buffalo."

"So they can be slaughtered by Mr. Rutherford and his rich friends? Thomas, excuse me for saying this, because I do believe you are a fine young man, but I could never pray for this quest of yours. I hope you never find them."

"If I don't, someone else will. Either way, they'd be killed for sport. At least I'd save a prize bull for Colonel Cody."

"But doesn't it leave a bad taste in your mouth to think that the great buffalo slaughterer himself could have the last free buffalo?"

Thomas' cheeks burned. "What's done is done. I had no part of it. All I want now is to help you get what's coming for the Indians and then, as soon as Sally can travel, we'll be on our way."

The Reverend said nothing more after that and went to

gather horses for their return to the agency post. Thomas stepped into the tepee and found Sally waiting for him. She still looked weak, but he saw an excitement in her face she could not hide.

"Come sit down beside me. We have to talk a moment."

"I ought to help the Reverend hitch up the wagon."

"That can wait a few minutes," she said. "I've just learned something very important to us."

Thomas hunkered down on his heels. What could Sally possibly have found out sick in bed?

She studied him so closely he began to squirm under her gaze.

"Well?" he demanded.

She seemed to reach a decision. "I *can* trust you, can't I, Tom?"

"You know better than to even ask."

"I'm sorry. Force of habit." She leaned closer and whispered softly, "I think I know where we can find the buffalo."

If she'd told him the sky was falling tomorrow, he couldn't have been more surprised. After all these months of searching, and now. . . . Thomas relaxed—of course, she was addled by fever.

"You don't believe me!"

"Sure, I do," he lied.

Sally eyed him skeptically. "Are you feeling all right, Tom?"

"Just fine." He decided to humor her. "Where are these buffalo?"

"Tame Doe won't say—exactly. Only that they are near a place called the Wind River."

"That's way south of here."

"Which is perfect for us! Tame Doe says the buffalo

herd is located right in a hidden mountain valley—like the one where we found the longhorns."

"And she'll draw us a map?" Thomas' heart quickened with expectancy. Tame Doe would not lie about such a thing.

"Even better," Sally whispered. "She has sent for an old hunter who has seen the buffalo this spring. He will lead us to the herd."

Thomas was overwhelmed. "That's more than we deserve. I . . . . I feel almost guilty about this, with the Crow nearly starving. Why don't these people round them up and drive the buffalo onto their reservation?"

"Buffalo aren't cattle to be herded. Anyway, the Crow believe Winfield would figure out a way to get them. They need our help."

In a way, Thomas was relieved. If this tribe was going to tell them something this important, they deserved horses or whatever else he could give them. "I'm listening," he said eagerly.

"She wants the blankets they have coming from Winfield. Without them, many will freeze this winter."

"I'll steal them if I have to. What's the second favor?"

"Tame Doe says you must kill the Indian agent."

"What!"

"Oh, dammit anyway," Sally stormed, "all I can do is repeat what she said."

"I don't believe you!"

"Quit shouting! Get control of yourself before the entire village hears us. Besides, you don't *really* have to kill him if you don't want to—just figure out how to run him off. We both know he's a murderer from what he's already done to the Crow."

That part was true and, in all honesty, Thomas had been

wondering if there was some way to rid the Crow of this
. . . this parasite who was bleeding these people to death.

"Will you do it?" She gripped his arm. "Thomas, she's
not asking for anything except justice. She told me they've
tried everything to have that man replaced. The Reverend
himself has even gone all the way to Washington but he's
never had any proof."

"There must be some records."

"I think Winfield alters them. I'm sure he's a clever
man, but there must be some way to trick or scare him
away."

"Did Tame Doe say how many buffalo were in the
herd?"

"She thought about a hundred. But does it matter, after
the way these people have shared the last of their food with
us, taken us in and asked for nothing?"

"No," he said, "it doesn't. I'll find a way, Sally. I'll think
of something."

"That's the spirit! I'd help you myself if I wasn't ill." She
coughed almost sedately to illustrate her condition.

Thomas shook his head. "I'd better go now." He paused
at the tent flap. "I talked to the Reverend about the buffalo. He wasn't very happy. I'd guess Tame Doe had never
mentioned them until now."

"They were a secret, but the tribal council gave her per-
mission to trade them for the sake of their starving people.
Winfield must go."

"They could get another Indian agent just as bad. Does
she know that?"

"I think so. But they really have no choice, do they?"

"I guess not." He lifted his head. "No, they don't have
any choice at all."

"I think you can do it," she told him. "You're smart, too.

You figured out how to get me away from those cattle rustlers."

"I'm not sure yet if that was smart or not," he said, unable to keep from grinning.

Sally laughed and he sure liked the sound of it.

Thomas fretted about the Indian agent all morning, trying to think of some way to get rid of the man once and for all. He didn't have enough money to buy him out and yet the agent's greed was his most obvious weakness, the one he'd have to use to trap him.

But how? What made things even more difficult was that Winfield had already seen him and would suspect anything out of the ordinary. As he and the Reverend rode back toward the trading post, he had the string of rustlers' horses as trade bait, but Winfield might not want them. Then what would he do?

"You've been awfully quiet," the Reverend said. "Something wrong?"

Thomas decided he had to have Jones' help, though he thought he knew the man well enough to guess he'd balk at using lies on Winfield.

"I understand you've gone clear to Washington to try to get a new Indian agent."

"I have. Did Tame Doe tell you that?"

"Yes. The reason I ask is that we need your help right now if I'm going to have any chance of trapping that thief."

"Go on."

"We'll set a trap of some kind to play on his greed."

"The Lord commands, 'Thou shalt not lie.' "

Thomas sighed. "He also says, 'Thou shalt not steal or

kill.' Winfield's doing both to your people. Sometimes, Reverend, strong measures are necessary to fight evil."

"Yes, but. . . ." He stopped and pointed off into the distance. "Look, a man on foot is coming up from the river."

Thomas stared in disbelief. "It's Moose Mulligan!" he breathed.

"A friend of yours?"

"He was. I think he still is."

"I wonder why he's on foot clear out here."

"I don't know," Thomas mused, though he could guess that Moose and Franklin Pierce had had a falling out. "He could help us."

"Do you think so?"

"I do." Thomas waved at Moose, who shielded his eyes, then gave a whoop and came striding in their direction.

Thomas chuckled. "Reverend, I don't know how, but Moose Mulligan is the kind who makes things happen fast."

Reverend Jones said nothing but, when Thomas glanced sideways at him, he was sitting up a lot straighter and there was a shining expectancy in his soft brown eyes.

CHAPTER 8

"Well, I'll be damned!" Moose roared with delight. "If it ain't young Thomas Atherton from Boston!"

Thomas leapt from the wagon and shook hands with the huge old buffalo hunter. He looked around for Franklin Pierce but didn't see him. "Where's your partner?"

At the mention of Franklin, Moose's smile died. "We split up," he growled. " 'Bout two months ago, we had a parting of the ways up near the Canadian border. He fell in with a gunfighter—an old-timer I thought I could trust. They both turned me out cold. All I have now is my rifle and these clothes I'm wearing."

"Well," Thomas said, "I've got a few extra horses, as you can plainly see."

"Can't pay for one," Moose warned. "You still looking for a buffalo herd?"

"I am."

"Humph," he grunted. "I thought you'd probably have given it up and gone back East."

Thomas shook his head. "I don't quit that easy. Besides, there's a herd waiting out there somewhere."

"Not in Montana. And them Canadian police sure as hell weren't going to let us shoot any legal. Pierce did anyway." Moose shook his head. "That fella sure changed. We got drunk one night up in Virginia City and he told me his family didn't want nothing more to do with him. They kicked him out with only a couple thousand dollars, which he's spending on women and whiskey."

"Franklin Pierce?" Thomas knew he was mean, but he'd no idea Pierce had been disinherited.

"The same. You wouldn't recognize him. Tell you something else—he's a killer. Shot a man, but the judge ruled it was self-defense. It wasn't. Pierce started the fight, then drew and shot the poor devil before he had a chance to even reach for his gun."

"Where'd he learn to draw and shoot a pistol?"

"From that gunfighter I told you about. He's practicing all the time. Says he's got a bullet with your name on it, Tom."

Thomas frowned. He was decent with a rifle because he needed to be able to shoot game. But he'd barely used the Colt at his side. Maybe, he decided, I had better learn to handle it, too.

Thomas decided to change the subject. "You've walked a long ways from Canada."

"I like walking," Moose replied. "Afoot, you can see tracks better and you're less likely to be spotted by Indians."

"You still think there are any wild buffalo left?"

"Sure do! The only question is—who's going to find 'em first and get all that money?"

"It'll be me."

Moose snorted. "Ha! It'll be me, boy!"

Thomas saw no need to argue. Time was running out as they were nearing the agent's post. "Moose, how would you like to earn a horse today?"

"One of your'n?" he asked skeptically.

"Yes."

"Why, shore. I like to walk, but it's still a hell of a long ways to Cheyenne. What do you want me to do?"

Thomas hopped off the wagon and motioned his friend to do the same. "Reverend, you just hold up the wagon a few minutes while Moose and I bow our heads together in prayer."

"Prayer, indeed! You're conspiring."

Thomas shrugged and, as Moose fell in beside him, he began to conjure up a plan.

Moose leaned down from the wagon. He felt trapped as he always had in an Army post. "And you say this Winfield is the Indian agent and he's got a place just down the road?"

The army sergeant nodded. "Maybe he'll give you a fair price for those horses, but we can't."

"Much obliged," Moose said, doffing his coonskin hat just as nice as you please.

The sergeant felt bad. "Them sure are good horses, but if the captain said no, there's not a thing I can do to change it, mister."

"Ain't your fault," Moose said, driving off with Thomas' string of trading horses following right behind.

A mile away, concealed in trees, Thomas sighed with relief. "He's done it. Here he comes now."

"How'd it go?" Thomas asked Moose when he pulled up. The trees hid them from view from the army post.

"So far, so good." Moose spat tobacco. "Only thing is, what if the Indian agent don't want to buy horses?"

"He will if you'll sell them cheap enough."

"It'd be a lot cleaner just to shoot the thieving rascal and be done with it."

"I could never allow that," the Reverend said.

"Some folks," Moose drawled, "always got to complicate things."

The Indian agent waddled over to Moose. "Those animals are in pretty bad shape. Two of them aren't even sound and a third hasn't enough wind to run around a tree."

"They got here just fine." Moose glanced nervously toward the hills and planted his bait. "You been having any Indian trouble lately?"

The agent bit. "Some. Guess you know all Indians love to steal horses. It's their nature. Part of their religion, even."

"That a fact?" Moose said, registering alarm.

"Sure is. Now, about those horses."

"Worth forty dollars each anyplace in Montana."

"Not without a bill of sale, they aren't. Just tell me the truth," Winfield asked seductively, "you stold 'em, didn't you?"

Moose fidgeted in silence.

"You don't even have to say it—just tell me where from."

"The Big Horns," he grumbled. "I wasn't followed."

"You can't be certain."

"I might take thirty dollars each," Moose offered hopefully.

"Twenty."

"Hell no!" Moose stormed. He began to climb back onto his wagon seat. "I'll take my chances of being robbed."

The Indian agent wasn't about to let him get away. "Hold up a damned minute. Could be I might swap you something for those horses."

"Swap what," Moose asked, trying not to sound too hopeful.

"Sugar. Flour. Provisions." He shrugged. "Whatever I got extra."

It wasn't what Moose wanted to hear. He needed something that could be identified as part of the Indians' allotment. "How about farming tools?"

"Uh-uh. Got some fine wool blankets, though."

Moose shook his head. "Don't want no damned blankets. They get all soggy if it rains."

"Then spread them out on the prairie to dry. That won't hurt them. Tell you what, I'll trade you eight dozen even for your string of crippled-up horses."

"How many is that?"

"One hundred, and you can sell them for a dollar and a half apiece in Cheyenne. You'll come out of this with a big profit."

Moose scratched his beard. It didn't pay to seem too eager, but he wanted to close this deal and be on his way. "I reckon at least I wouldn't freeze to death it if snows."

"Of course, you wouldn't. And I'll tell you this," Winfield said with a sly wink. "If you're really smart, you'll head up to Virginia City and hang onto these until there's a blizzard. Hell, then you can turn around and sell them to those shivering miners for ten dollars each!"

It sounded like such a fine idea that Moose was half tempted to actually do it. A hundred blankets at ten dollars each had to be nearly as much as the herd of buffalo would bring. Not that he couldn't still hunt them next spring.

"It's a deal," he said, weighing all the angles. "A man has to look out for whatever he can get in these hard times."

The Indian agent smiled. "Brother, I couldn't have said it better."

"Here he comes with your blankets," Thomas said. "I told you he could do it!"

They stood up and watched the distant wagon come angling across the prairie. Thomas felt proud of himself for coming up with the idea and just as proud of Moose for pulling it off. Now, all they had to do was wait until Winfield showed up at the fort trying to sell the horses. That's when they'd roll the wagon in with the blankets and make their case stick. The army didn't need to know the Indian agent had been set up by his own greed.

Suddenly, the wagon stopped, then turned around.

"What's he up to now?" the Reverend asked with sudden concern. "Why is he changing direction? Look, he's applying the whip!"

Thomas' mouth dropped open. "Damn him, anyway!" he howled. "A man can't trust anybody out here!"

It wasn't until the bundles started breaking open and blankets began to sail off the wagon in every direction that Moose pulled in the team of horses and abandoned the idea of getting rich in Virginia City. By the time they overtook him, he'd reloaded everything.

Thomas was in a killing frame of mind, but the Reverend was full of forgiveness. "The Lord called you back to us," he proclaimed. "He broke the twine and gave you the chance to redeem yourself, Mr. Mulligan."

"Reverend, you are a wise and saintly man who can see into a fella's heart and know the straight of things. As God is my witness, the Devil possessed my whip hand but the Lord's power was pullin' the brake handle."

Thomas groaned but let it pass. He wasn't fooled for a minute; the truth was, Moose had decided to take the Indian blankets and head for the hills. It was disgusting, but he was glad he'd learned the man's true character. A few hours ago, he'd half decided to bring Moose in as a full partner—but not anymore. One thief was enough to deal with without adding a second.

They pulled the wagon around and headed back to Winfield's trading post. They'd done all they could do—now, it was up to the Indian agent.

They didn't have long to wait. Less than two hours later, the agent passed down the road to the army fort leading his newly acquired string of horses.

"Sure didn't take him long," the Reverend said. "He is a greedy man.

"In a couple of hours," Thomas added, "he's also going to be in a real fix."

Now that the trap had been sprung, the Reverend did not waver. "The Lord will punish him for the suffering he's caused among the Crow but, until then, I hope the army imprisons him until he's an old, old man!"

Thomas was a little surprised at the venomous edge in Reverend Jones' voice and yet he could not imagine how many Crow Indians would have died of hunger and suffering this winter without their full complement of food and blankets. If it were up to me, Thomas thought, I'd order the man before a firing squad.

Moose climbed back up into the wagon. "Guess there's no sense in giving the man any more rope to hang himself with. By now, he's probably gone to the captain and tried to sell him the same horses I did."

"I wish I could be there to hear him explain *that.*"

Thomas chuckled. "And I'd give anything to be there when you arrive to sell these new Indian blankets."

"Some fellas get all the fun." Moose winked. "But if either of you showed up, they'd know it was a trap from start to finish. Me, I'll just look dumb and happy and send him to prison."

The rest of that afternoon was the longest Thomas could ever remember. The Reverend spent it in prayer, but Thomas just kept watching the fort through the trees and wondering what could be going on. He kept worrying that maybe the captain and the Indian agent were both thieves and everything would blow up in Moose's face and that maybe *he'd* be thrown in the cell. And if that happened, what would they do—what could they do—for Moose? Freeing Sally had been difficult enough, but breaking Moose out of an army jail would be impossible.

"Have faith," the Reverend kept saying.

But Thomas had none. He'd prayed off and on all his life but nothing he could see had ever come of it. The Lord was either too busy or enjoyed watching people dig themselves in and out of one fix after another.

The sun was sliding into the western hills and firing up the sky when Moose drove out of the fort.

"Look at that, will you!" the Reverend cried. "You see what he's got!"

"The horses. It means they gave them back to him and took the blankets. The whole army post is our witness. You'll have those blankets tomorrow. I'd bet on it."

The Reverend fell to his knees and bowed his head in silent thanksgiving, and Thomas said his own quick words of gratitude. He just knew things would get better now for the Crow and that he'd had some small role in seeing that they did.

Maybe, he thought, praying isn't useless and maybe my luck will turn now that I've finally done something right.

Moose said later that they'd thrown the Indian agent into a miserable little detention cell to await the arrival of civilian authorities, not expected until spring. As for the blankets, they were delivered by an army patrol led by the captain himself, who told the Crow leaders *they* could decide who'd be their next Indian agent.

Sally and Thomas took long walks every day for a week so that she would be strong enough to leave when they'd go to hunt the buffalo.

"Can you sense the hope in them now?" Sally asked him one afternoon.

"Yes. I wonder who the tribal council will pick as Winfield's successor."

"The Reverend, I'd guess."

Thomas thought so, too. The council had been going on for almost the entire week. Indians did not make quick decisions, especially when they dictated their very survival. And though he'd never before been invited to a tribal council, the Reverend had explained that the Crow, like most Indians, did not act on a majority rule. Everyone had to agree or nothing was done.

Moose sauntered over to join them. "These things can go on for months."

"The Reverend has told them they have to decide today. They need a new agent right away."

"They'll pick him, then. You can bet they would anyway, but they'd like to jaw and smoke their pipe around on it until spring."

"How do you know so much about them?" Sally asked.

"I was married to a Sioux and I've lived with most tribes long enough to understand their thinking."

"You were a squaw man?"

"I was. And proud of it," Moose said. "Winona was the best woman I've ever known."

Sally nodded. "I meant no offense. What happened to her?"

"Doesn't matter anymore," Moose said abruptly.

The tribal council was over and the first man out was the Reverend Jones.

"He looks pleased," Thomas observed.

The Reverend strode over to them and he was smiling broadly. "Well, it has been decided."

"Congratulations," Moose said, extending his hand.

"And the same to you, Mr. Mulligan. I know you'll do a fine job."

Moose staggered. "Me! You're crazy!"

"Perhaps, but the Lord told me your heart and spirit were with these people. You're a big, strong man and you've already saved us."

Moose hadn't sufficiently recovered to argue yet, and Thomas used the opportunity to grab his hand and pump it hard. "You're perfect!"

"But . . . but what am I supposed to do!"

The Reverend's voice was soothing and confident. "The Lord never gives us a task we cannot handle. Moose, you will never be alone in this."

"But I *like* to be alone."

"Nonsense. Your job doesn't pay much in worldly remuneration, but. . . ."

"How much *does* it pay?"

"Seventy-five dollars a month."

Moose swallowed drily. "I've earned more than that in a good day of hunting."

"The job will not be an easy one."

"It won't?"

"I'm afraid not. You must be a spokesman for the Crow and a peacemaker. In your reports. . . ."

"Whoa up, there. I can barely read 'n' write!"

"By spring, you'll be well schooled. I promise you that much of an education. The federal government is convinced we ought to become farmers. Unfortunately, our Montana summers are too brief. If the Crow are to survive, it must be from raising livestock, sheep and cattle. This is grazing land, not farmland."

Moose took a deep breath and expelled it slowly. "Yep," he conceded almost reluctantly, "I've always thought that, since the Plains Indians are the finest horsemen in the world, they could raise, break and train horses to sell to the army and ranchers."

The Reverend clamped his frail hand on Moose's powerful shoulder. "That's a fine idea! Perhaps we could sell them as far south as Cheyenne or even Denver."

"Santa Fe even," Moose said. "We could breed us a little stouter horse, one strong enough to pull a wagon."

"But retain the Indian pony's stamina."

"You bet," Moose said. "Them little suckers can run for hours and hours. There's only one thing, though."

"What's that?"

"Seventy-five dollars sure isn't much." He scratched his beard, winked at Thomas. "Don't suppose you could ask the tribal council if I could get me a pretty squaw in the bargain?"

The Reverend wasn't amused but obviously sensed this wasn't the time or place for a lecture on morality. "I'm sure that where the seeds of love, trust and respect are planted, there will be a fruitful harvest. And there are, as I'm sure you've noticed, a few such women who admire your strength and bravery."

Moose hesitated a moment and then blurted, "What does Goes Walking think?"

Sally interrupted. "She likes you, Moose."

"How do you know?"

"A woman can tell in ways you'd never guess. She watches you when you don't see her."

"She does?" He swelled up his barrel chest with pride. "That's a pretty woman. How come she's got no man?"

"She's a widow. Her husband died in battle two years ago. She is still of childbearing age."

Moose cleared his throat and toed the dirt. "I may be a little old for that, Reverend, but I do like her looks."

"Then I'll make the arrangements."

"For what?"

"For you to move in with her after the marriage ceremony."

"Now, whoa up! This is all movin' sorta quick, ain't it? Besides, I intend to find some buffalo first."

"You've hunted them already. They brought you nothing of lasting good. Goes Walking can and will bring you happiness and you, in turn, will help her people."

Moose looked at Thomas almost as if he were begging him for help, asking for some good reason to ride his new horse out of this camp and country as fast as it could carry him. But to where? Cheyenne, where old buffalo hunters like himself withered in rocking chairs on boardinghouse porches and then died forgotten paupers? Or to the boomtowns, where he'd be too old and stiff to swing a pick all day in a hellhole of a mine?

"Do it," Thomas urged without hesitation.

Moose looked away to the blue forever skies. "There's buffalo out there. I can feel them in my bones. I can smell 'em in a high wind a hundred miles away. I could find 'em, by God!"

"I believe you. But then what? After the money was drunk up and gambled away, what would be left?"

The fierce light in Moose's eyes bedded down a little and the old hunt fever slipped away to leave him questioning. "You're a hard man, Tom."

"Nope. Just honest. You'd never be happy sitting in a front-porch rocking chair. Out here is where you belong."

Moose knew he was right. He scratched his beard, then grumbled, "I promised Cody I'd send him a buffalo bull the size of a damned log cabin. Gave him my word on that."

"I swear I'll send Cody the best I can find."

"What about this Cyrus Rutherford fella?"

"He'll have to be content to shoot the second best."

"You could be riding into some bad weather this time of year. If you and Sally get stuck in a blizzard, you both might freeze to death."

"That's the risk we take. Nothing is free. You know that."

Moose had obviously about run out of arguments, though it was clear he wanted to go along. "You better watch out for Pierce and that damned gunslinger friend of his named Otis Elwood. They want your hide. It ain't only your life that's at stake, it's the girl's."

Thomas nodded somberly. He'd told Sally all about Franklin Pierce, how he'd been disinherited and turned killer in Virginia City. Thomas had known Pierce for years and the man had always been possessed of a vicious and slightly crazy nature. More than once they'd almost come to blows over Pierce's cruel treatment of a horse or a hunting dog. Thomas knew he could whip him with his fists, but probably not in a stand-up gunfight.

And this Otis Elwood made Thomas' stomach knot with worry. It was a damned good thing for the West that the day of the quick-draw artist was nearing its end. When right or wrong meant nothing compared to one's skill with a six-gun, justice just naturally went out the window.

Thomas looked Moose right in the eye. "I'll tell you this much," he said in a hard, flat voice. "If we see them, I'll have my rifle in my hands and I won't hesitate an instant to use it."

"Good!" Moose said. "Now yore thinkin' like a man who wants to live awhile longer. Tell you what, I'll show you how to use a buffalo rifle. That way, you can kill 'em before they even get into their own firing range."

Thomas nodded. It seemed cold-blooded, but he'd be damned if he'd take any chances with Sally's life.

Tame Doe's mysterious warrior had finally arrived to lead them to the last wild buffalo herd, just as she'd promised. Their silent escort was, she explained, an outcast, a man who'd fallen in love with a married woman and then fought and killed her jealous husband, who'd attacked him without warning. For this, he'd been banished for seven years to wander alone.

Thomas had the impression the man was a Crow, but he never spoke the language—in fact, he never spoke at all and communicated by sign. Tame Doe said his name was Three Knives, and that he was brave and loyal. Cast out by the Indians, he had become a mustanger after a few years but lived only to end his years of banishment when he could return and marry the woman he loved. Thomas thought him and his life's story absolutely fascinating.

It was hard to say good-bye to the Crow Indians, harder still to keep Moose Mulligan on the reservation when he discovered their mission. And yet, now that Winfield was gone, he had much to do in his new job as Indian agent.

At the crown of a hill, Thomas gazed back to see the old hunter standing almost a foot taller than anyone in the Crow village. And though he wouldn't have admitted it aloud to Sally, he wished the man were riding side by side with them to the Wind River country. That, just one last time, Moose could see and hear the free-rolling thunder of a herd of stampeding American buffalo.

CHAPTER 9

The warrior rode day after day, always about twenty yards ahead. By the second afternoon, they'd covered over a hundred rugged miles and Thomas was convinced that he and his pony were as hard as steel, as tireless as a steam locomotive. He did not know what the pair of them ran on—only that they never stopped to rest unless asked. They would start at dawn and end at sunset when he and Sally were so weary they could no longer sit upright in their saddles.

Three Knives never pushed a fast pace yet his pony could trot almost forever on nothing but water and a little brown prairie grass. They skirted the Big Horn Mountains and passed into a huge, arid basin. Thomas found himself tying his coat to his saddle in the afternoons, though it was still cold at night. At the end of the third day, they camped by an enormous hot springs and Sally was ready to spend awhile recovering from saddle sores.

"This is it," she declared. "I'm going to go sit in one of these hot pools and soak for a week."

"I don't think Three Knives will wait."

Sally eyed him cooly. "He's completely worn us out and damn near killed our horses. Who's running this show, us or him?"

"Him," Thomas said without hesitation. "You know it as well as I do."

Sally frowned. She knew it was true and she'd already

spent no small amount of time trying to charm Three Knives into slowing the pace. Failing that, she'd given him a piece of her mind but he'd paid her no attention whatsoever, which made her furious.

"I don't like that man!"

"Don't waste your energy" was Thomas' advice. "Save it for tomorrow."

That night, they soaked for hours in the steaming hot pools and enjoyed it immensely. All their aches and sores vanished and, by scooting toward or away from the pool's center, they could regulate the water temperature until it was just perfect. Overhead, steam rose as if from a witch's cauldron and, as the night wind shifted, they got a view of one constellation after another.

"I could almost winter here," Sally told him dreamily. "Wouldn't it be something to lie and watch the snow fall into these clouds of steam and never feel the cold?"

Thomas raised his hand and studied it closely. "Maybe, but we'd come out as wrinkled as a used-up chaw of tobacco."

Sally's brows knitted with annoyance. "For cripes sake! Here I am talking about something nice and . . . and lovely even, and you say a thing like that. Thomas, I just have to say this, you sure know how to squash what little romance there is in this life."

"What's romantic about your skin being all white and wrinkled?"

"Never mind! I'll bet you and that Alice Rutherford have a lot more in common than you think."

"What's *she* got to do with anything!"

"You're still in love with her, aren't you?"

"I guess," he said dubiously. "It's been a long. . . ."

Sally wasn't even listening. "I'd just like to meet her

some day and see what you think is so high and mighty special about the girl. How can you love somebody you haven't even kissed? Even held hands with or . . . done anything to?"

She was making him squirm in the steamy water. "I don't want to talk about Miss Rutherford. You just couldn't know about a girl like that."

Her eyes glinted. "You mean someone rich, well educated, cultured—a damned debutante!"

"Yeah." He clenched his teeth in anger. "All those things."

"Oh," she warned, "it might just surprise you to know I am very familiar with that kind of people—the upper class, as we referred to ourselves in Philadelphia. Ah-ha! I see I've your full attention now."

Thomas was ready to get out of the hot pool, dry off and go to sleep. They could sit here until midnight, but it was a cinch Three Knives wouldn't care if they slept or not. At daybreak, he'd throw his Indian blankets across the knotty backbone of his skinny, iron-legged pony and go riding on until he came to the buffalo. Thomas knew he should leave now, yet something told him that, finally, he might learn something about Sally's mysterious past, a past he'd been dying to uncover ever since he'd first met her on the train that night rolling across the Nebraska plains. But, on the other hand, she might just as likely begin another one of her silver-tongued lies.

"Well," she decided out loud, "I just get kind of weary seeing you moon for a girl you don't know."

"I don't 'moon' over anybody." He was getting mad.

"What else would you call it? Your entire reason for coming out West was to make yourself worthy of sweet Miss Alice."

Thomas struggled for self-control. "We were talking about *you*, Sally Whoever-you-are. You and Philadelphia."

"Me, huh. All right. Not that you or anybody else gives a damn, but I was once a proper young lady, Tom. My father was a lawyer, his father was a lawyer and it went right back that way to the War of Independence. The Winslows of Philadelphia were an old and respected family of lawyers. My father was rich, handsome, successful—exactly as he was supposed to be. Had I been a man—and to his dying day he blamed me for not being one—I'd be a lawyer, too."

Thomas studied her face intently. This time, he'd stake his life she was telling the truth. "So what went wrong?"

"Everything." Her voice dropped to a whisper. "A law partner ran off with nearly a hundred thousand dollars in trust money for which my father was liable. My mother then broke under the strain when he couldn't raise all the money and the newspapers caught wind of the story. You know, the weak love to bite off the legs of the strong."

"And he fell?"

"Almost," Sally whispered. "It was a terrible blow; he felt he'd disgraced generations of Winslows, ruined the family name. Not that I cared. But, do you know what?"

Thomas shook his head.

"He still would have made it, through everything, except for my brother, his only son. My brother Andrew was born mean. There is no other way I can explain him. I could tell you stories that would turn you cold inside, but I won't. It's enough to say that Andrew was thrown out of law school for cheating and then he set fire to the administration office. He sort of went crazy and, less than a year later, they arrested him for the murder of a woman of ill repute in Trenton."

"Did he do it?"

"My father couldn't believe that he had, but then he'd never really admitted how twisted Andrew was and how vicious when drinking. Father was blinded by love and thought his only son could and would become a prominent lawyer and live to redeem our family name. Being a girl, I could never do that."

She leaned her head back and let her hair touch the water. Thomas gazed longingly at the soft curve of her throat, her chin and those lips he could remember kissing.

Sally tried to smile but failed. "I'll make this tragedy mercifully short and spare you all the scandalous details. Suffice it to say that my father bribed a witness to protect his boy and was caught. It was over. He was disbarred, disgraced. Two days later, he shot himself in our library. I left on a stage even before the funeral."

"And your brother?" Thomas dared to ask.

"Andrew was eventually tried . . . found guilty of murder . . . and executed."

Thomas took a deep breath. He was numbed by the story. Absolutely numbed.

"Let's go," Sally said roughly as she climbed to her feet. "I don't know why the hell I told you all that anyway."

She started to turn but Thomas caught her wrist and pulled her close. "I think you told me because you love me," he said, feeling her body tense like a coil.

She struggled and he knew how she could fight if she really wanted to, so he added, "Now I'll tell *you* a secret, I don't dream about Alice anymore. I dream of you."

She froze in his arms. Her expression of pain and outrage melted and, when they kissed, Thomas felt a shiver jolt him clear down to his wrinkled-up toes. He didn't know what Sally felt, only that her lips touching his made fire and, for now, that was enough.

On the fourth day, they climbed up a rib of the Big Horns and, judging from the way the Indian pushed his horse, Thomas knew they were very close to the valley of the buffalo.

Below them, the great Wind River Valley nestled like a warm mother-cup surrounded on all sides by blue, white-capped peaks.

The forest grew dense, the air almost cold after the warmth of the valley floor and then, suddenly, the trail vanished into a mountainside and they were riding under a plume of water into a mountain tunnel. A short way inside, Three Knives dismounted. They watched him carefully un-wrap a bow and a quiver of arrows from a buffalo hide that had been tucked into a rocky crevice. He strung the bow, remounted and stoically continued on. Their horses' hooves drummed on mossy rock and the air grew damp and chilly. Thomas glanced back to the sliver of waterfall, realizing it was at its lowest and, most of the year, would hide this entrance completely.

Perhaps three hundred yards ahead, the tunnel dog-legged and there was a glow of daylight. When they reached it and turned, the light grew bolder until, finally, passing long-dead campfires, old bones and broken pottery, they reemerged into the fullness of day. They were in a long valley, sheltered on all sides by rugged mountain peaks. The grass beneath their horses' hooves was lush and almost velvety.

Three Knives gave a high, primordial cry and drummed his moccasined heels against the pony's rib cage. The animal jumped forward, plunged through some pine trees and startled the finest herd of buffalo imaginable.

"Look at them!" Thomas shouted as they galloped on. "There must be a hundred!"

Beside him, racing neck and neck, Sally rode like the devil was on her heels. "We're going to be rich!" she cried. "Rich!"

They got the buffalo herd running and chased it for nearly a mile before Three Knives motioned them to rein in their horses. Thomas simply could not believe the size of some of the bulls! There were at least five who were larger than any of Cody's.

They dismounted and let their horses blow. Sally's eyes danced.

"Look at them, Tom! I never dreamed I'd see them running wild, heads down and swinging, tails up and flying. They look so much better running free."

He couldn't argue the point as he watched how the bulls, with their enormously powerful forequarters, slung their heads about and flared their nostrils. He was reminded that smell and hearing were their only real defense. The irony was that nothing living could smell or hear 550 grains of hot, screaming lead.

"How will they kill them?" Sally asked quietly.

Cyrus Rutherford was a purist, a man who favored tradition over convenience. "Probably the same way they used to. Cody said he'd slip up to a bunch like this and carry a forked stick to prop his rifle barrel. It saved his arm and, when the barrel grew too hot, it wouldn't burn his hands. Then, he'd make what he called a 'stand.'"

He glanced sideways at her. "There's not much point in thinking about them as anything but money, Sally. If we don't use this opportunity, someone else will eventually discover this valley and slaughter them for their hides."

"What's a stand?"

"I don't know. That's just what Cody said. He'd lie downwind and shoot the one who looked like the herd leader. Usually it was a cow, often with a calf."

Sally's lips formed a thin, unforgiving line.

Thomas pushed on to finish the story. "Then another leader would take its place. Come over to the dead cow and make noises, try to rile up the others. Before it could get the herd running, he'd shoot her, too, and just keep dropping them as long as his rifle could fire."

"And they didn't do anything. They just stood there?"

"Yeah. They'd start milling around. Bulls stomping and shaking their heads until they were all finished."

Sally's expression was puzzled. "I don't understand things sometimes. Like why God made something that proud and fine-looking so stupid."

"They just weren't made to face a man and a rifle, I guess."

"That's no answer. If God created them, he must have known this would happen."

Thomas didn't have an answer to that either. "All I can say is that they were here thousands, probably millions of years. Their time was up. It's our turn now. Things are always changing."

"Look!"

He twisted around to see Three Knives raise a bow and arrow to the sky and call out a word that sounded like "EE-OWWAAA!" And though the temperature was only in the fifties, he was now stripped to his breechcloth and moccasins, with a sheath knife in his belt and the quiver of arrows slung behind his shoulder with a leather thong.

"What's he going to do?" Sally asked.

"He's going to kill a buffalo the way the Indian has for centuries."

"But they're worth over fifty dollars each to us!"

"Do you think he cares how much they're worth to someone like Cyrus Rutherford and his rich friends?"

"No, I guess he wouldn't," she replied, watching intently.

Three Knives and his buffalo pony approached the wary herd. The pony wanted to charge; Thomas was horseman enough to see how excited it was and yet how perfectly controlled as it rigidly held a steady gait. The bulls snorted and pawed, bunched to form a ragged line between themselves and the cows. Suddenly, at twenty yards and without any apparent warning, a bull lowered its horns and charged.

Thomas' heart skipped as the pony dodged with the quickness and agility of a puma and then darted fearlessly into the herd, miraculously avoiding the slashing horns. Its defense penetrated, the herd fragmented as if an explosion went off in its midst. The animals stampeded in all directions and, out of the pack, riding straight and tall, came Three Knives.

He was magnificent and, with his pony running flat out after the cow he'd chosen, Thomas knew he was seeing a very, very rare exhibition of skill and horsemanship. As the pony drew closer to its quarry, Three Knives leaned in on the cow until the tip of his drawn arrow was but inches from its chosen target.

"I can't watch," Sally whispered, "and I can't *not* watch!"

Thomas understood perfectly. The drama being played before them spanned the centuries: this was the curtain call and Three Knives knew it deepest of all. His lean body twisted, the muscles in his back corded powerfully, his arms and his shoulders were ridged splendidly until the very moment when his bow unleashed its deadly missile. The cow's head snapped back even as its body folded in upon itself and the beast collapsed and cartwheeled in a dusty tangle of hide, horn and blood. The cow thrashed in death only a moment before it lay still and Three Knives came to stand triumphantly beside his kill. His face reflected a mixture of wonder and respect, joy and even a trace of sadness for the animal which had always given his people the means to live.

The buffalo thundered on to the edges of the valley and then waited in a silence broken when the Indian threw back his head and called out something only he and his god now understood. The echo rolled around and around the canyon, then finally escaped to the hills and valleys on and on.

Thomas saw the sheath knife flash, and he turned away to look down at Sally. In one day and one night, he'd learned more about her than he'd dreamed was possible. Now, he could read her eyes, see all the protest rising inside of her to spill out of control. Thomas wanted to stop her first. Maybe he didn't care about impressing Alice Rutherford or her father anymore, but he still wanted the money and the stake in life this herd would give them.

"They're doomed," he told her in a flat, emotionless voice. "They're stupid creatures not fit for this world."

"You don't believe that."

He had to appear sure of himself if he were to be of any help at all. "Yes, I do. Sally, it's not as if these were the last buffalo on the face of this earth. There are other herds. If these die, they won't become extinct."

"Perhaps not!" she argued with passion. "But this is the last *free* herd in the world. I've heard you talk about Cody's buffalo. You've seen them. They can't be the same. Not anything like these!"

He would try a different line of argument. "Someone will slaughter these animals someday and we might as well be the ones who profit. Besides, you've said from the beginning that all you cared about was the money. Well, here it is!"

"To hell with Rutherford's money," she said coolly. "We can make it some other way."

"How? By stealing wallets and watches?"

The moment he said that he could have cut out his tongue.

Sally looked away for a moment and when she turned back to face him her voice was ragged with pain. "You win. We'll telegraph Rutherford and tell him he and his friends can come for the slaughter. But *you* will have to kill the very first one."

Sally yanked the Henry rifle and shoved it hard against his chest. "Take it!" she demanded. "If you can shoot one, then so can I."

His fists clutched at the rifle "We'd be losing a hundred dollars," he said, not really giving a good goddamn.

"Three Knives can tan the hides and the rest doesn't matter. You can even shoot one of the calves; they can't be worth anything to Rutherford and his gang of butchers."

She was being completely . . . completely unreasonable, so he took the Henry and marched across the valley feeling mad as hell at the both of them. They'd come a long, hard way to this point and now, when they'd finally gotten some luck and actually found what they'd been searching for, Sally had gotten softhearted.

Sally! The last woman in the world he'd have thought would turn down the opportunity to make a small fortune.

Well, he thought angrily, one quick bullet would end all this stupid sentimentality. He'd been shooting pronghorn antelope and deer for supper; he sure didn't believe these buffalo rated any better treatment.

Thomas spotted a cow and a calf he guessed to be about six months old. The cow was cornered between some rocks and a fallen tree. Her faulty little eyes blinked at them with a vague and distracted fear.

"You shoot the cow," Sally said without any sign of emotion. "I'll shoot her calf."

He nodded stiffly and kept walking. "This isn't a buffalo rifle. I want to get as close as I possibly can. One shot through the heart or lungs. No suffering."

Thomas moved to within thirty yards of the cow before he sensed that, if he came any nearer, she would charge. He stretched out on the hard ground and brought the Henry to bear on a spot just behind her forelegs. He still couldn't do much with a pistol, but he knew he could kill the cow with a single, well-placed bullet.

The seconds ticked by. Overhead a fly droned, and he let it distract his concentration. The cow was starting to quiet a little, yet he noticed how she kept crowding her calf back behind herself for its protection. He wondered if the cow had even the haziest sense of her own futility and impending death. For some reason, he was reminded that back in the big Eastern cities, rich people raised orchids in moist little hothouses all year around despite the plant-killing winters. These Wind River buffalo weren't pretty like hothouse orchids, but they'd been just as protected all their lives in this secret paradise canyon.

"What are you waiting for?" Sally challenged. "Go ahead and shoot."

Losing his temper, he squashed the trigger and the rifle boomed. Smoke blossomed out the barrel and the lead slug ricocheted meanly off the rocks. Thomas dropped the rifle in self-disgust and rolled to gaze up at Sally, who stood with her hands on her hips looking very pleased with things.

"I'm a lousy shot."

"And a worse liar." She knelt to cradle his face. "Let's save this herd, Thomas. Our hearts aren't in the killing. If Buffalo Bill Cody needs a prize bull, then let's give him one and make him pay for it dearly. One of these top bulls ought to be worth five thousand dollars if it's worth a cent."

"I don't know about that," Thomas said dubiously. "The Colonel has seen thousands of buffalo running wild. Could be he's not going to be so impressed."

"There's only one way to find out and that's to deliver one to the East and see what happens. If the Colonel doesn't want to pay our price, there will be dozens of rich men like your Mr. Rutherford who will gladly do so in order to own the *last* free bull buffalo. Think of the publicity it would bring!"

She was absolutely right. Some men would pay any price to have a certain distinction.

"The problem with all this," Sally mused, "is obvious. How do we get a bull clear down to the Union Pacific line?"

Thomas thought about it carefully. "We could rope and drag him to the railhead."

"*You* could rope and drag one. Look at their size! The big ones outweigh two horses. They look stronger than oxen."

"Then we'll have to drive him to Rock Springs."

Sally's brow furrowed. Her blue-green eyes studied a bull who stood poised across the valley. "I don't think they will cooperate," she said quietly. "I think we are going to have a hell of a time making any of them leave this place. But you're the expert."

"With horses, not buffalo." Thomas picked up the rifle and they trudged back. "I watched Cody's buffalo for only a few hours, but I did see them used in the Wild West Show where they were driven, in a matter of speaking."

"What does that mean?"

"It means they move in the general direction you want, but I got the impression they could be as stubborn as mules and as dangerous as grizzly bears."

"I'd guess it's at least a hundred miles to Rock Springs. That's a lot of provoking, Tom. Maybe we ought to try the carrot instead of the stick."

"We don't have any."

"Buffalo bulls must crave something."

Thomas colored slightly. "Only one thing I can imagine and we can't dangle that around."

"Tom!" Sally marched on ahead, pretending indignation. But he knew she wasn't really angry and, to be honest, he doubted a buffalo bull would chase anything else.

The good part was that they had two strong ropes tied to their saddles; the bad part was they didn't know how to use them. Of course, they'd both seen cowboys lasso horses and cattle, but watching was a far cry from doing.

They'd practiced roping for the better part of a week, first on rocks and bushes then, when they'd mastered the basics, on each other and, finally, on their poor horses.

Three Knives had thought the entire affair quite amusing and Thomas supposed it was, if you had no stake in the outcome. Thomas had no doubt he understood their motive, perhaps even snatches of their English. The Indian had witnessed Thomas' off-the-mark shot at the cow, and his attitude toward them had improved tremendously since. At first, he'd only watched as they spent hours practicing with the loops. At last, he'd shown them how to build a proper loop, hold the rope and swing it overhead, then flick it out with a snap of the wrist so that it dropped down on its target and could be jerked up tight. He was infinitely patient with them both and never seemed to mind that his lessons were taking him from his own task of preparing the hide and smoking the buffalo meat. Three Knives had eaten the tongue and hump fat right away and that was fine with Thomas and Sally, who soon grew weary of buffalo meat.

Actually, if fall weren't nearing its end and winter coming right behind, they'd both have enjoyed their stay in the valley. The fishing was good, the crisp, bracing days a delight and the nights . . . Thomas had never dreamt there could be such nights. He and Sally were going to wed. Theirs would be a passionate but sometimes turbulent marriage. The problem was nobody could tell Sally anything, and he guessed he wasn't much better taking orders himself.

But now, as they saddled their horses and prepared to go out and rope a ton of fighting hide, hair and horn, he wondered if they really had any chance of succeeding. He thought they could each rope the beast, but it was what would happen next that had him mighty worried.

"I guess this is it," Sally said in a tight voice. "Wooly Bully?" It was the name she'd affectionately given the largest, finest bull in the herd.

"He's the best of 'em."

"Then let's get him," she said with determination.

They caught Wooly Bully off guard down in a wallow. Every day, they'd ridden at him until he scarcely bothered to watch. Now, as they swept in fast, he was almost yawning as they began to swing their loops. By the time he'd climbed to his feet, shook the dust from himself and pawed his warning, Thomas was sweeping in and making his throw. The rope sailed out perfectly—but missed!

Sally was right behind and as Wooly Bully spun and hooked, she laid her rope as pretty as you please over his head, dallied her horn and swerved off to the left. Wooly Bully didn't understand ropes and when this one clamped down on his windpipe and yanked him off balance, he managed to bawl with unmitigated outrage—then to get even.

He threw his weight against the rope and Sally's horse choked to a shuddering halt. The bull shook its massive head and shoulders as the horse fought to keep its balance. Thomas gathered his rope just as fast as he could, cursing himself every second. The bull fought Sally's rope like a whale on a line, and Thomas knew it was going to charge her any minute. Sally would let go of the rope; they'd made that decision going in when they'd agreed not to tie it fast to their saddlehorns and risk having a horse gored to death.

"Hang on!" he yelled, spurring back in with his rope looping a hard, flat circle overhead.

Wooly Bully charged Sally. Thomas drove in from the huge animal's rear and, this time, he was on target. When the buffalo struck the end of his rope, Thomas thought he'd lassoed an eastbound freight train as he was running west. That buffalo almost turned him and his horse inside out. His saddle was twisted around sideways and his horse knocked off its feet and dragged. Only his years of riding and his own quick reflexes kept him from being crushed by his thrashing mount as it tried to clamber to its feet. Thomas heard Sally shout a warning. He turned to see the bull lunging toward him and then, like a blur, Three Knives was in the middle of everything. He drove his pony forward with a yell and Thomas stared in disbelief as he threw himself on top of the buffalo. Sally had prevented the bull from making a quick charge, but she couldn't hold on much longer with her rope. Three Knives must have realized someone was going to be killed if he didn't act because he'd whipped off his jacket and now was slamming it down over the bull's horns, right up through the armholes. He jerked it down over the bull's face, blinding him totally.

Wooly Bully froze in baffled fear. He began to toss his head about wildly, then spin around and around until he tired and, head down, stood panting and helpless.

Thomas' horse clambered shakily to its feet and they tightened their ropes on opposite sides as the warrior lashed the blindfolding jacket in place. Wooly Bully offered no resistance.

"EEE-OHH-WAA!" he bellowed. "EEE-OHHH-WAA!"

Thomas looked at Sally. Her expression reflected his own shock and amazement.

"We've got him," he said quite simply.

"I know."

"We're going to get him to Rock Springs."

"I know that, too."

"And when Cody buys *him*, I'm going to buy *you* a wedding ring."

She just bit her lip and nodded. There wasn't a thing more either of them needed to say. Not even to Three Knives, who had obviously read their thoughts and hearts from the very beginning.

The talking was over. It was time to deliver their magnificent Wooly Bully. He'd make the headlines back East.

CHAPTER 10

Getting their buffalo out through the mountain tunnel had been the toughest part. Already blinded by the leather jacket, Wooly Bully initially hadn't panicked in the darkness, but the cavernous echo of hooves on rock had made him freeze, then bolt and run like hell. They'd had their ropes on him, of course, but the damp rock floor was as slick as ice and they hadn't even been able to slow his frenzied charge.

He probably would have run a couple of miles if not for the cave's dogleg. The poor, half-crazed beast had slammed into the moss-covered wall like a runaway locomotive. Thomas heard the impact, felt the mountain shake and quaked fearfully as pebbles rained down upon them.

Sally was more concerned about the buffalo. She ran forward calling its name as they heard it moaning like a cow in hard labor. Thomas also went to the aid of their fallen prize. Other than being groggy and in considerable pain, the bull seemed only temporarily damaged, for neither its horns nor its neck was broken. However, when Wooly Bully hadn't risen after nearly twenty minutes, Three Knives impatiently grabbed the bull's tail and gave it a sharp twist.

Wooly Bully jolted to his feet as if struck by lightning and, five minutes later, they were outside once again, breathing deeply of the cool fresh air and blinking like owls in the light of day.

It was time to say good-bye and Thomas, still not certain if Three Knives fully understood English, tried anyway. "We won't be returning to this place," he promised because it was important. "Sally and I realize now that the buffalo herd belongs to your people, not ours."

Three Knives just reached out and touched each of them on the arm. Thomas thought of it as a benediction and figured maybe it would help make their journey ahead an easy and ultimately profitable one.

The Indian bent back his head and howled softly, almost mournfully and then he trotted away. Thomas watched him vanish over a hill, moving like a well-oiled machine.

"He sure likes to yell a lot," Sally said, "but I'll miss him anyway."

"So will I." He tugged on the rope. "Come on, Wooly Bully." Since running headlong into the rock wall, the animal had become very hesitant to charge forward—he wasn't going to make the same mistake a second time.

Their trip to Rock Springs was uneventful except for a cold storm that brought sleet and made travel miserable the last two days before they arrived at the railroad stockyards. Once there, however, the word quickly spread about the huge buffalo who allowed itself to be led into the loading pens. Within hours, hundreds of townspeople arrived at the yards to gawk and admire a creature whose kind had once roamed these very hills and valleys by the millions.

Old men who remembered how the buffalo had rolled across the grasslands like a lowland tide just stood beside the big wooden holding pen and reminisced about a better time when they were young and, like the buffalo, figured they'd be around forever.

Kids reacted differently. Most of them wanted to know all about how the buffalo had been hunted and how Thomas and Sally had managed to tame such a monstrous bull to be led like a tame dog.

Some men saw the chance to make money and, within the first hour, at least a half dozen had offered to buy Wooly Bully. Two planned to exhibit him in sideshows, but the rest intended to cut him up into tiny pieces and serve him at an exorbitant price, because when else would a person ever have the chance to eat buffalo meat?

Thomas and Sally turned down every offer, explaining patiently that this one was for Buffalo Bill Cody's Wild West Show.

Everybody seemed to accept that part of it just fine and so they telegraphed Colonel Cody in Chicago, where Thomas had learned the show was playing. They asked Cody for five thousand dollars and said, truthfully, that every old-timer in Rock Springs had agreed that Wooly Bully was a prize bull, young and strong. Within a couple of years, Cody's herd would be blessed with new size and vigor and would be worth far more than it was now in its present state of inbred debilitation. And they asked him to send enough money for Sally and himself to accompany the bull back East for their honeymoon.

"I don't want to return to Philadelphia," Sally told him.

"There's no reason you need to," he said, taking her arm. "Let's go down to the telegraph office and see if the Colonel has accepted our offer."

"Do you think he will?"

"I do."

"But what if he doesn't?"

"Then we'll have to take one of the local offers."

"And have him cut up into little meatballs and sold on street corners?" Sally was horrified by the idea.

"Then what do you suggest?"

"Either we take him back. . . ." When she saw Thomas' expression cloud up, she added quickly, ". . . or keep him to exhibit ourselves. We could charge people two bits apiece to see him in a tent."

Thomas thought that was a lousy idea and said so. "Everybody's already seen him for free."

"Then we'll go to Cheyenne. Denver. We could make a living off of good old Wooly Bully! You could sell tickets while I work the crowds."

Thomas was appalled. "No wife of mine is going to be a pickpocket!"

She giggled impishly. "Relax. I was only kidding." As if to prove it, she playfully jabbed him in the ribs. "Anyway, it's very nice to know you don't want to marry me just for money."

It was a sensitive issue and one he failed to find humorous.

At the telegraph office, they were disappointed to find that there was still no answer from Cody. They walked back outside, feeling discouraged.

"Maybe he's already left Chicago," Thomas mused. "If he has, it could take days to track him down."

A voice, cold and mocking, answered, "Try Baltimore, if you can afford the price of another telegram."

Thomas stiffened and turned to face Franklin Pierce.

This man bore little resemblance to the one he remembered from Boston. Then, he'd seen the meanness, but it had been half-buried under the facade of wealth and the rules of proper social behavior. Now, all that had been cleanly stripped away to reveal someone much stronger, much more utterly himself. It occurred to Thomas that, had Pierce not been disowned, he might have gone through life choking back his ruthlessness or merely feeding it small cruelties, like the beating of dogs or horses, the stomping of ants and roaches when no one was watching. All that had changed with the territory and the circumstances. Disowned, he'd been thrust into a fire and found it to his pleasure. And with the hard life and a fast gun, he'd tested himself in battle and his veneer of softness had melted away like suet until he was tempered steel.

All this, Thomas knew in a moment. He'd seen strong men crumble under the weight of a tragedy in just a few days; it did not, therefore, surprise him in the least to discover that the opposite also could be true. No, he wasn't surprised, just suddenly wary and very careful, because he knew he was gazing at the face of a killer.

"What are you doing here?" he asked quietly.

Pierce's fish eyes weighed him and he was slow to answer. "I found a herd," he said with lowered voice. "And now I've gotten a telegram from Mr. Rutherford."

Thomas tried to hide his surprise and keep his voice steady. "Where did you find buffalo?"

"Who is the girl?" Pierce asked, wetting his lips and letting his eyes slide up and down her length so provocatively that Thomas' hands knotted from the desire to choke the lust from him.

"She's going to be my wife."

"My, my, what about Miss Alice!" He feigned astonishment and alarm but it was a child's game, one Thomas would not play.

"You can have her if she's stupid enough to take you, which she is not."

Pierce's smile froze, then melted into twisted hatred.

"We'll see. She's coming to us, you know. Miss Alice, in case you never realized it, likes to see men compete for her favor."

He barked in fits of laughter that made the hairs on Thomas' neck rise.

"As I said, she is all yours," Thomas repeated.

"Maybe," Pierce suggested with a wink, "I don't want her either."

Thomas didn't know how to respond to that one. Pierce's eyes seemed to burn in their sockets. He had grown a wild beard and his entire manner suggested that he was dangerously out of kilter, out of control. The very last thing Thomas wanted was to draw against him. Not only would he probably forfeit his life, but he was afraid for Sally. Pierce could not seem to take his eyes off her.

"So," Thomas said, "you found a herd."

"No, *you* found the herd. We just followed your trail back to that valley. Quite a place, isn't it?"

Despite the temperature, Thomas was sweating. "Is that where your partner is? At the valley?"

"Uh-huh. He's waiting. Lots of meat and some whiskey to keep him happy until I bring Cyrus and his friends."

"Those buffalo belong to the Indians. I won't have you bringing Rutherford and his bunch here to destroy them."

"I'm afraid, Thomas, you can't very well stop us. If you draw on me, I'll kill you. If you ride back to that valley, Otis Elwood will kill you. Or you might get lucky and kill him, saving me a lot of money."

He lowered his hand to rest near his gun. The invitation was chilling and clear. To draw against him would be suicide—Pierce knew that. And yet, to just walk away and be followed by Pierce's mocking laughter would cut away Thomas' soul. So he did what he could. He planted his boots and swung his fist at that leering face just as hard as he could.

Too late, Pierce's own fist dug for the gun at his side. Just as his fingers gripped its handle, Thomas' knuckles smashed against the point of his chin and the smile on his face shattered like glass. He backpedaled into the wall and Thomas punched him in the stomach, then knocked him out cold with a chopping right hand to the side of his lean jaw. All together, the punches hadn't taken three seconds.

"Thomas, you were tremendous!" Sally cried happily.

He bent and rifled the unconscious man's pockets until he found the telegram. Thomas desperately hoped he'd been lying, but he had a sick dread inside that told him Pierce had spoken the truth.

"Is that it?" She knew exactly what he was searching for.

"Yes," he said, unfolding the telegram and reading it quickly. "And I'm afraid the Rutherfords and friends are provisioning themselves at this very moment. They expect to be here in exactly fourteen days."

"Miss Alice too?"

He read it more slowly this time. "Yes, but. . . ."

"Good! I won't marry you until you see her again."

"Don't be ridiculous," he said with impatience. "What we have to do now is save the buffalo."

"Only the Union Pacific or God Himself could do that, Tom."

She meant that their train would have to break down, but the company would just fix it or send another—and only God could bring on a prairie blizzard, one long and bitter enough to block travel until spring. But even if that did happen, what was there to prevent Rutherford from simply returning in the spring to slaughter the herd? Thomas knew the answer was nothing, absolutely nothing.

There were no more secret valleys, no more wild herds hidden protectively out of time. And even if there were, the full revelation of his find would send hunters and fortune-seekers stampeding into the most remote areas.

No, Thomas thought, the herd is doomed.

"We're not giving up on this," Sally told him angrily. "You may, but not me!"

"I'm not giving up."

"That's not what your face says," she told him, letting her anger out slow.

"You want to go back there?" He knew she did.

"We have to."

"The old gunfighter." Thomas placed his hands on her shoulders. "He won't let us near the buffalo. Not without a fight."

"I've thought of that. But we must try anyway. All my life, someone has wanted me to do something, or keep me from doing another thing. So, I've fought. I've lost more than I care to remember, but we have to fight in this world for the things we believe in. Otherwise . . ." She paused for a moment. "Otherwise, *we* are lost."

Thomas knew she was right. He was a fighter, too, only he couldn't have expressed the reasons nearly as well as Sally. But it would be so easy just to accompany Wooly Bully east. They could sell him, take their honeymoon and never look back. But they couldn't, of course, because the last wild herd in America would be slaughtered and they'd have done nothing to save them. For years, maybe their entire lives, they'd bear the shame, carry it as a part of themselves until it corroded their integrity, their self-respect and then even their love.

"All right," she said, "let's go make arrangements for Wooly Bully and then clear out before someone gets shot.

If he shoots you, Tom, he won't live to tell anyone about it." Sally wasn't boasting or threatening or anything, but just stating a fact. Thomas really didn't know quite what to say so he kept his mouth shut. All he knew for certain was that a lot had gone wrong in the past ten minutes. Up until then, he hadn't thought past getting married and taking Buffalo Bill's money. Wooly Bully was a bargain at that price, worth every cent of five thousand dollars and, though that wasn't a fortune to the likes of Rutherford and his crowd, it was enough to build a dream for their own futures.

But now, Thomas thought dismally, he faced no less than a professional gunfighter, a herd of very uncooperative buffalo, a crowd of rich Eastern shooters who'd come chasing after them led by Franklin Pierce, who'd certainly want to kill him—and, Miss Alice Rutherford, just the vision of whom had made him weak in the knees since they'd been kids. Not that he believed she had any powers over him now, but he had to admit the thought of seeing her made his stomach knot up like a rawhide ball. He wanted to see her again, just to show her—and himself—that he no longer cared.

It seemed strange and all wrong to be riding north again, straight into the teeth of a freezing wind. Overhead, the sky was a gray slab of suspended marble, cold and unyielding. Their horses, already thin, moved with their heads down low, ears slicked back in protest. They were worn out, cantankerous and balky. At night, they were hobbled and tied because they would have turned their tails south and drifted.

It snowed on their third day out and still they pushed on until the horses refused to go into the face of the storm any longer. Fortunately, they found cover in some trees and made camp beneath a latticework of sticks and branches.

Through the long night, the wind moaned and the snow hurled itself across the land while under their shelter Thomas held Sally close and warm. That night he dreamed of buffalo and Indians and, once again, saw the hidden canyon. It was sundown and the sky was crimson, the valley snow-covered and glistening like a bowl of polished silver.

Thomas groaned in his sleep. Now came the buffalo and the Indians, and they were marching in a military column of four abreast—two buffalo flanked by two Indians. Hunters waiting to shoot lay crouched holding rifles longer than their bodies. Thomas tried to shout a warning but the only sound other than the wind was the soft crunching of snow underfoot as the Indians and buffalo marched unswervingly toward their extinction.

Thomas agonized over the sheer inevitability of the scene as it unfolded and felt that nothing, nothing in this world could stop or even alter the course of events he was about to witness.

And he was right. With a cry frozen on his lips, the rifles boomed and the first four tumbled and began to roll. While he watched, four more were felled, and four more again. Thomas could not watch any longer, yet he wondered where they would all go, how far they could roll.

Sally was shaking him awake. Saying words that didn't matter except that they drove the nightmare far back into the darkest corners of his mind.

Thomas shivered. "I'll find a way," he vowed, "I swear I'll find a way."

"We both will," she whispered. "Together."

Thomas tasted deeply of her mouth, felt the warmth of his own blood pounding in his ears. He felt his heart beat faster and stronger and knew that she was right—somehow, they would save the damned stupid buffalo.

The morning broke clear. Thomas looked up at the weak morning sun and stretched his ropy muscles. They saddled their horses and rode over bright, crusted snow until early afternoon, when they approached the canyon and paused to consider what awaited on the other end of the tunnel.

Finally, Thomas dismounted and tied his horse in the trees. Sally did the same, and he wished she wasn't so head-strong. He pulled out the Henry rifle. "We'll catch this Otis Elwood by surprise."

Sally nodded, checked her pistol and the derringer she carried hidden inside her boot top. She was obviously ready for anything as they hiked toward the cliff and the secret tunnel.

Inside the tunnel felt steamy, almost hot, though it wasn't. At the dogleg they halted, and then Thomas pushed Sally firmly behind him and lifted the rifle. He could smell smoke. His hands felt clammy and his feet seemed as heavy as buckets of rocks. He had never killed a man before and the prospect of doing so now was not ap-pealing. Still, he reminded himself once more that he could not dare hesitate to shoot if shoot he must.

Elwood was a gunfighter, and that kind of man did not survive very long if they waited to ask questions. Foot by foot, they edged forward until the shadowy figure of a man crouching beside a fire loomed just ahead. He was just a rectangle of darkness and he was very alert. Thomas saw him move like a flash and even as he raised his rifle, he wanted to shout a warning yet knew he had to shoot now or he'd be dead.

The Henry blasted through the tunnel like a cannon. His

bullet screamed off rock and then something like fire knocked him spinning and the agony was indescribable.

Sally's gun barked over and over in answer. Thomas folded to his knees, trying to raise the Henry once more. His hand caught on something foreign. He reached down to his side and, as his mind strained to hang onto reality, he felt an arrow.

"Three Knives!" he shouted hoarsely. "It's Three Knives!"

Sally waited until the echoing gunfire rolled out into the canyon before she whispered, "Oh dear God, I hope I didn't kill him."

He tried to say something. Do something. Instead, he was overcome by the pain as the darkness came flooding in.

"It looks worse than it is and you lost more blood than a stuck pig, but Three Knives didn't seem worried that you'd take poison and die."

"Small comfort there," he gritted.

"Cheer up," Sally said, kissing him quickly. "Three Knives has gone back to the Crow Reservation for help. You can be sure Moose Mulligan will come, too."

That *did* give him comfort. Maybe, he thought, things would work out somehow. He looked up at her. "Never thought I'd wind up getting shot by an arrow. Not with the Indian Wars over. Has Three Knives finally started talking English now that things have reached this sorry state of affairs?"

"Nope, we talked in sign language. I told him that a big party of hunters was on its way."

Sally reached over to a low burning fire and turned some buffalo meat on a stick. "I don't think the Crow are going to let anyone slaughter their buffalo herd."

"Rutherford has always taken what he wanted. They may not have a choice. The men won't go back empty-handed and in defeat."

"You don't think he'd go so far as to actually open fire on the Indians if they stood in the way."

Thomas wasn't sure. He'd seen Rutherford on hunts and the man was imbued with such enormous conceit that he'd never be able to back down to the Indians. There was a lot of General George Custer in Cyrus Rutherford. His pride, his enormous self-confidence would tell him he could defeat the small band of Crow and, perhaps, even immortalize himself in the bargain. He'd have all the advantages. The Indians would be illegally absent from their reservation and, when it came to arms, they would be hopelessly disadvantaged with their old single-shot rifles, their outdated bows and arrows.

Thomas shuddered to think of how lopsided a battle between the rich Eastern hunters and the impoverished Crow would be. Why, with their telescope-mounted, custom-made big game rifles, they'd be able to finish off the Indians before they could even get into their effective firing range!

He remembered the nightmare—the irreversible end of the buffalo and the Indians—and it caused him to sweat with dread.

"Thomas! Are you all right?"

"Yes," he managed to say. "But we've *got* to leave this place, Sally. Leave before it runs red!"

When Thomas felt able to walk, they soon discovered Elwood's body right where it had fallen. The man had been skinning a buffalo, or at least attempting to. Less than a hundred yards away, three more carcasses lay dusted by

snow, two cows and one healthy young bull. Clearly, Elwood had killed them just for sport.

On a day when the weather turned unseasonably mild,
he and Sally inspected the canyon and discovered that it
had a concealed opening now blocked with fallen timbers
placed so skillfully a rider could pass within eighty feet and
never notice the canyon hidden beyond.

"That's it!" Thomas knew this was the break they'd
been needing; it would have been almost impossible to
drive the herd through the mountain tunnel.

"Now," he said, "we just have to figure out a way to herd
them across the prairie."

"I'm not sure we can. If Wooly Bully hadn't run straight
into the tunnel wall, we might still be trying to get him to
Rock Springs. Besides, you know they'll overtake us."

"Then we'll fight, but on our own terms. They have the
weapons, but they don't know this country and the cun-
ning of the Plains Indian."

"I agree," Sally said. "But you must have considered
what would happen to the Crow if they kill Cyrus Rutherford and his companions—even in self-defense."

Thomas knew what she was driving at. These were rich,
influential men; the Indians would be crucified.

"Thomas, the thing that's so damned sad about all this is
that even if we win, we lose."

He drew her to him and was surprised to feel her crying
softly against his chest. It hit him hard. For some reason,
he just hadn't thought she was able to cry.

Moose Mulligan and seven Crow warriors had slipped
from their reservation unobserved, leaving Reverend Jones
to devise a cover story for the United States Army. He'd
probably say that the Crow's horses ran away and they'd

had to go off to find them. Now, though, Moose was alive
with the excitement of fresh adventure. By his quick laughter, you'd have thought he was out to have a real good
time.

"Boy!" he said, grinning broadly as his eyes surveyed the
herd. "I told you there were some left, didn't I!"

"You sure did," Thomas agreed heartily.

"Damn right! I told the Colonel and everybody else too.
Jest look at them! Pretty a sight as I've seen in years. Makes
my trigger finger twitch."

Thomas suppressed a smile. "We're going to *save* them.
Remember that, Moose. Remember, too, that it's two hundred miles back to your reservation. We are running out of
time."

He nodded. "Let's get that pile of timber moved and get
out of here today. I've got a little surprise waiting to show
you."

"What is it?"

"Oxen," Moose shouted happily as he strode off to get
them. "And wait until I hitch them up and you see them
drag that wall out."

He was right. Later that afternoon, when they'd cleared
away all the timber and brush, Thomas and Sally finally got
their first chance to really admire two of the biggest oxen
imaginable. They were monstrous beasts who weighed an
even ton apiece. Without their power, it would have taken
an entire day to clear the opening; with their help, it took
less than two hours.

When they were all finished and Moose had let them
drink, Thomas walked up to him and said, "What are you
planning to do with them now?"

He winked knowingly. "You'll see. The real show is
comin' right up."

No one had to supervise or direct the Crow when it came time to move the wary buffalo. Leaping onto the backs of their ponies, whooping and yelping, they stampeded the buffalo down the canyon with the eager enthusiasm of children.

It was a hell of a sight! Thomas and Sally watched spellbound as the Indians drove the racing herd clear to the end of the big canyon, then turned the whole bunch around and drove them back again. Altogether, it was a good tenmile run and the buffalo were blowing hard and stumbling with weariness by the time it was over.

But the Crow weren't satisfied. They rounded the herd up and pushed them back for one more long run.

"They'll kill them."

"No they won't," Moose said. "Jest push them 'til their tails are dragging the dirt. Notice how they're starting to bunch up into a herd instead of all trying to break off into the timber? Even more important, they found the leader, that tall old cow up front."

Sally frowned. "What good is it going to do them?"

"You'll see. Watch."

Three Knives roped the lead buffalo neatly by the forelegs and she fell hard. Dazed, she never had a chance to fight off the Indians, who fitted her up with the neatest set of rope harness Thomas had ever seen. By the time the cow was allowed to regain her feet, the Crow had hitched her up to the pair of mammoth oxen. They didn't even twitch when the cow hit the end of her rope. Heavy lidded cud chewers, the oxen just stood their ground while the cow fought and squalled to free herself of the rope harness. The fight was short-lived and then the Indians led the pair of massive oxen along dragging the poor buffalo cow.

Moose grinned when the cow finally climbed to her feet

before all her hair and hide was scraped off and decided to cooperate. Motioning to the Crow, he headed toward their new opening. To Thomas and Sally's surprise, the herd docilely fell in behind their lead cow with the Indians prodding the exhausted stragglers. Once out of the canyon, they pointed them north down into the valleys.

Thomas glanced back at the canyon only once. It was sunset and the frozen waterfall mirrored a crimson sky. He gazed at it for a long time, then he turned his eyes forward.

That night the exhausted buffalo did stay on their bedground reasonably well, though no one slept very much. Just after dawn they were traveling again, the huge team of oxen setting a leisurely pace; the cow, fresh after a night of rest, fought for the first hour, then gave up and behaved herself like an everyday milker.

"Do you think we can make it?" Sally asked once again.

"I don't know. What day is it?"

It took her several minutes to figure it out and, when she told him, he was shocked. "I lost two days somewhere," he admitted. "They're closer than I thought."

"Those oxen, I could crawl faster than they walk!" Sally said with disgust. "How much lead time do you think we have?"

"Four days. Maybe five."

"With nearly two hundred miles to go. We're going to have to make a stand, Tom."

He had no answer because there really was none. With horses, that would be plenty of time. With a veteran herd of longhorns? Sure! But with buffalo . . . with buffalo, they might just as well be trying to outleg their pursuers to California.

There was no chance at all.

CHAPTER 11

That evening the temperature plunged, and it took them until long after dark to find a low bedground where a fierce, arctic-like blast could not scatter the herd. By midnight it was snowing hard, and the buffalo kept trying to drift south with the wind. The snow blew parallel to the ground, cold, blinding and unrelenting as Thomas, Sally, Moose and the Indians struggled through the long predawn hours to keep the buffalo milling together. Daybreak came late, a gray pallor giving precious little light, timid as a mouse, and threatening to leave them at the slightest provocation.

By noon, their noses and eyes ran icicles and the buffalo formed a walled knot; tails out, heads down, they'd dug in to wait out the storm.

The men also sought shelter. Behind their horses, they burrowed into a snowdrift, anywhere at all. By late afternoon, the wind's steady howl had abated and snow began to swirl. Thomas and Sally remounted their horses and knew they were lucky, because the storm could easily have lasted four weeks.

They wondered if it had turned back those who pursued them. Sally believed it surely had, but Thomas was certain that it had not. You just had to understand a man like Cyrus Rutherford. Thomas' father had always said that Cyrus was like a train: once it started rolling you couldn't stop it nor could you turn it around. Only thing you could do was either get out of its way or outrun the damned thing before it killed you.

He wondered if there was a little "train" even in Alice. Had she ever been denied anything? Had anyone stopped or outrun her? Thomas knew they hadn't. What he *didn't* know was how he'd react when he saw her again. That probably sounded weak and foolish, but there was no sense denying she still had a power over him. Besides, people always thought they knew how they'd react in any given situation—but they didn't. You could decide how you *should* react, tell yourself exactly how you *wanted* to react, but when it came to fear, love, hate and all the rest, your heart, Thomas thought, decided what you did, not your mind. And you couldn't trust the heart. Not all the time. Hearts were as fickle as debutantes, as changeable as the weather. At least up until now his had been. Hell, just months ago he'd sworn he'd never love anyone but Alice, and then he'd fallen for Sally.

Sally was freezing cold. With her face buried deep in her fleece-lined jacket, her hat pulled low, all he could see of her were those big, penetrating eyes that seemed to read his thoughts at the exact moment of their formulation.

Did she know he feared Alice almost as much as he did Pierce or Mr. Rutherford? No, he decided, for if she did, she would not love or respect him.

Thomas reached out and brushed snow from her jacket. She pulled down her collar and said, "We're going to make it, Tom. We're going to beat them somehow!"

He nodded vigorously, feeling a surge of pride in her and a boost in his confidence. She was right. One way or the other, the Crow were going to keep their buffalo and he was going to have Sally for his bride. He wasn't going to let this turn out any other way.

It snowed off and on for another two days, but after that initial blizzard it was nothing to them. Now, with the sky washed clean of the dark, brooding clouds, the earth seemed to shake itself to life and the temperature edged above the freezing mark.

To Moose's great disappointment, they discovered they no longer needed to harness the lead cow to the oxen. She was trail broke even to the point of seeming to enjoy her new responsibility. They turned the oxen loose to fend for themselves until someone could return for them. It was extremely unlikely that the huge beasts would be attacked by anything in its right mind.

Without the oxen, they doubled their pace the next two days as they followed the Big Horn River north. Passing the hot springs, they watched the big steam clouds pillar up into the sky, and both Thomas and Sally gazed longingly as they remembered this as the place where they'd finally given up on their hurt and resentment and let themselves fall in love.

Out of the basin they pushed, skirting the Big Horn Mountains now mantled with a deep, fresh snow. Twenty-five miles to the east, Custer and his men lay resting under the frozen ground—legends, like fools, often die hard.

How far did they have to go? Forty miles? Closer to fifty. Another day? No, the buffalo were growing cantankerous. Pushed too fast, they were beginning to whirl and charge their tormentors. A day and a half then.

Thomas kept dropping back and moving to the high places where he could watch their backtrail. "Where are you, Cyrus Rutherford?" Thomas asked the land that rolled out before and behind him. "Where!"

That night, big Moose caught his eye and beckoned

Thomas to follow him out onto the moon-drenched snow. He was pensive, his usual rough banter gone.

"What is it?" Thomas asked anxiously.

He filled an old briar pipe, tamping it carefully, then lighting it before he spoke. When the match struck, Thomas glimpsed an expression on Moose's face that he'd never seen before. It was a very old face, one as brown and wrinkled as cracked shoe leather, a face that had stared into the sun much longer than it should and had been pelted by ice and washed by rain. It had been beaten by fists, licked by dogs and kissed by a few good women and a lot more bad. The face was abused, scarred, busted, even kind of lopsided but it spoke volumes for the man who owned it. And tonight, it looked terribly, terribly old.

"What do you think about me being the Crow Indian agent, Tom?"

The question surprised him but his answer came easy. "You'll be good. The best ever."

Moose shrugged. "I don't think so," he confessed. "While you were gone, some army brass came out to the trading post. They gave me a stack of paperwork. Things to buy, reports to write, a plan of goddamn action to put down. I told 'em to shove all of it."

Thomas groaned. "You shouldn't have. Why didn't you ask Reverend Jones to help you?"

"I dunno. I don't like to depend on people to do my job. Never have, never will."

"You can learn," Thomas urged his friend. "We can always learn."

"*You* learn," Moose said. "I'm too old to change my thinking. Besides, come spring, I'll want to roam."

"Not if you take a good squaw for a wife."

He snorted. "I'm too old for that, too. Tom?"

"Yeah?"

"I think you ought to take my job next spring."

"Don't be ridiculous!"

"I'm not. You coulda stood up to them officers. Written their damned reports and such. You'd be good at it. Real good!"

"Forget the idea. Sally and I are getting married. She wouldn't be happy up there."

"You don't know half of what she's like yet. Might be, she'll surprise you."

"Might be," he agreed. "She always has."

Moose brightened. "Good. You jest think on it awhile."

"I will, but my answer won't change."

Moose smoked in silence for several minutes as they listened to a pack of coyotes howl. He looked sideways at Thomas. "You see them just before sundown?"

He didn't have to ask who. It was understood. "How far back?"

"Not more'n a few miles. They had to see us earlier on."

Thomas shook his head. "Then there's no use in running."

"None at all. But I do have a plan."

"I'm listening."

"First off, you probably won't like it but it would solve our problems in a hurry."

When Thomas said nothing, Moose continued. "What I want to do is take the Crow and attack, at daybreak. With any luck, we can kill the bunch of them before they can fire a shot."

Thomas stared openmouthed. "I can't believe my ears!" he croaked. "You'd kill them all!"

"Better them than maybe us," Moose said in an injured voice. "Dammit, Tom, there ain't no Eastern rules of fair play out here. That's the way the Indians would do it, same as the cavalry if they were outnumbered. We could bury the lot of 'em and nobody would be any the wiser. Come spring, they'd be feeding the wildflowers."

"The hell with that!" Thomas swore. "If there's killing, let the blame be theirs, not ours. I'll tell you something else, those men came all the way out from Boston. Their families are rich and powerful enough to make life hell for the Crow, and I'll guarantee you we'd all hang for our trouble. Besides, there's a woman among them."

"Damn," Moose growled, "that does change the picture. I never shot a woman yet and I won't begin tomorrow morning. But I'm telling you, I'm not about to let them people use their fancy rifles to pick us off one by one."

"They won't. We can always give up the buffalo."

"Won't ever happen."

Thomas thought it over. The idea of simply letting themselves be overtaken wasn't pleasant. "I understand the Crow are great horse thieves."

"All the Plains Indians are. To them, it's an art, a part of being a man. What do you have in mind?"

"Just thought they might like to get in a little practice tonight."

Moose grinned. "They would at that!"

"Good," Thomas said decisively. "Wake me when you're ready to leave."

"I want to go, too," Sally whispered as the sound of Moose's boots crunched off through the snow. "Thomas, I won't stay here."

He held her close. "You don't have to," he said evenly. "You and four of the Indians are going to start moving the buffalo."

"But if you steal their horses, then why?"

"Just in case."

"In case *what!*" she demanded. "They can't catch us on foot."

"I know," he said patiently, "but they are not stupid people. There will be a guard. They must know we're camped up ahead."

"So, you think there will be gunfire."

"Anything is possible," Thomas admitted.

Sally sat up with her blankets pulled tight against the cold. Her expression was filled with worry. "We have come a long way together. First time I saw you on the train, I thought you were a natural-born sucker, just ripe for the picking."

"And I was." It seemed like a hundred years ago.

"Almost. But when you stood up to Rodney, him with those crazy eyes that could scare people half to death, and when you tried to make me feel better, I knew you were special."

"But you took my money anyway." The words had spilled out unintentionally. It still hurt to think about it, but that was in the past. Past hurts were about as useful as old newspapers—everybody knew the only thing they were good for was wrapping dead fish.

Sally swallowed noisily. "I didn't know how to handle him anymore. I was afraid of him, Tom."

"You could have left him. He had no hold on you." His voice trembled. "I still can't see how you could have loved such a man."

Sally struggled to form her next words. And when they came, Thomas was stunned. "He was my brother, Andrew. I loved him."

He took a deep breath. *Now,* it made sense. All of it. "Is he the same one that killed that woman in Philadelphia?"

"He's the one they said did it," Sally admitted with her chin up. "He swore he was innocent, of course. Father and I believed him. Then. Later, when he killed a man in Cheyenne, I knew we'd made a terrible mistake and he was a murderer. That's when I left him . . . to . . . hang. It was that day we raced out of town. It took me a long time before I could get over the anger and the guilt."

Thomas watched tears roll down her pale cheeks and then he cradled her face in his hands. "Why didn't you tell me he was your brother? It ate at me to think he was your husband—or lover."

"Being my brother made it worse. Lots of people think that viciousness runs in the family blood. And you *thought* I was a murderer just like Andrew. Don't deny it."

Her eyes were faintly accusing, and he knew there was no sense in denying anything. "Maybe I did at that. I wasn't sure of anything. Then, when you suggested we kill Winfield at the Crow agency, I was afraid you were. . . ." He couldn't put it into words she'd understand.

"A murderess."

He nodded. What a fool he'd been!

"It was partly my fault. I shouldn't have made that crack about the Indian agent. But I was boiling mad. And I was testing you to see if you still thought I was so terrible."

"You're a hell of an actress, Sally." He took a deep breath. "And I *am* a sucker. I believe most anything people tell me until I get hit between the eyes a few times. I'm the guy who rode out believing you really could speak all the Indian languages. Remember?"

"Sure do," she said with a mischievous smile on her lips. "Maybe I was pretty foolish to tell you that. We could have gotten into some terrible fixes. But let's be honest with each other from now on. I want you to admit you may be going out tonight to do something just as foolish."

"I don't agree. If we can steal their horses, the chase is over. We've won."

"It's not that simple. We both know that." Sally looked away. "For example, what if your Alice Rutherford can't make her way back to Rock Springs on foot? She and the others could die in a blizzard or just starve to death out here this winter. They might get lost in the snow and suffer frostbite and lose fingers and toes. Could you allow that to happen?"

"No," he said grudgingly. "I couldn't. We'd have to help them. But not until the buffalo are on the Crow reservation and protected from harm." Thomas pulled his boots on and crawled out of his blankets. "I've got to go now. You and the Indians should start pushing the buffalo as soon as you can. With luck, you can be at the post tonight. Not even Cyrus Rutherford would challenge the United States Army whose job it is to keep whites off Indian reservation land."

"But will they do their job?"

"If forced to, yes!" He was angry. It was time the army started living up to its responsibilities.

She stood and faced him. "I'll see those buffalo move along smartly until we get there. Don't you worry about us. Just don't forget that *I'm* the woman you're going to marry."

"I won't. I. . . ."

"Shhhh." She placed a forefinger on his lips. "No promises. I don't need them. Now go on, Tom, and learn how to steal horses. Never can tell, it might come in handy someday."

He turned and left. Seeing him smile as he strode toward the horses, no one would have guessed how deeply worried he felt inside.

Franklin Pierce had learned a few things in his months of buffalo hunting. He'd chosen to camp right out on the prairie where the ground was as flat as a billiard table and, in the light of a full moon, even a stalking coyote would have been highly visible. His party had pitched their tents in a tight circle.

But the Crows didn't seem concerned at the lack of any cover. They rolled around in the snow until it caked their buffalo robes. They even packed it into their hair until they looked like backyard snowmen.

"It's a long ways to crawl," Moose said. "Are you sure you're up to it?"

Thomas nodded. "You just cover us and if there are any surprises use my rifle."

"Too far to their camp. Have to use my old Sharps buffalo rifle."

Thomas eyed the big-bored weapon in Moose's hands. "I'm hoping you don't have to use either. But they could be expecting us."

"I doubt it. They'd never imagine anyone could sneak across that much flat snow."

Thomas reluctantly wrapped a blanket around his shoulders and got down in the snow and rolled until his teeth were chattering but he was covered with the stuff.

Moose was enjoying the display yet had a ready piece of advice. "Let the Crow do the hard part of getting those horses. They're the experts. You just be close enough to back them up with that six-gun."

"I'm still not very good with it," Thomas said. "I'd feel a whole lot more confident with a rifle."

But a man crawling along through a gutter of ice and snow hasn't any room to carry a rifle, so Thomas started after the Indians, who were already far ahead. He didn't go thirty feet before his teeth were chattering, and his hands and knees felt like lumps of ice.

Thomas dragged himself for what seemed like forever, trying to tell himself how lucky he was not to be breaking the trench like the men before him. He'd heard of Indian children and how they were taught from earliest childhood to block physical discomfort from their minds. Trappers and frontiersmen alike had often told stories of seeing almost naked Indian rolling down snowbanks like playful otter.

Well, Thomas thought, so I'm no Indian kid. My belly aches and growls when it's hungry, I sweat and get dizzy if I work too hard in the bright, blazing sun, and my teeth chatter in the freezing cold.

He tried to take his mind off his shivering body by thinking of Sally. How she looked and. . . .

A gun cocked. He stared down at a pair of boots and felt the icy barrel of a six-gun prod his forehead.

"That's far enough," Franklin Pierce breathed.

Thomas raised his head. There was still a good fifty yards to the picket line, but Pierce hadn't waited for them to arrive. He was alone. The Crow had their hands upraised. Their faces were without expression, though they probably figured to be executed.

"Get up, slow and easy."

Thomas felt a drenching sweat wash over his chilled body. He glanced toward the Indians and shook his head, hoping they would not try to run because Pierce would like nothing better than to shoot a trio of horse-thieving Crows in the back.

"I'm going to give you a chance," Pierce said. "You've always thought I had things so damned easy, had every advantage over someone of the working class—*your* class. Now, we are going to see who is the fittest."

Thomas was not comforted by this veiled offer. "What does that mean?"

Pierce was enjoying himself to the limit. "Only that Miss Alice deserves to see you beg for your life before I finally put an end to it."

He tried to act brave but it was a struggle. "You've been reading too many dime novels, Pierce. This isn't Dodge City and I've no intention of drawing on you."

Pierce shrugged, then pivoted on his heel, pointed his gun at Three Knives and cocked the hammer. The message could not have been clearer.

"Hold it," Thomas said, coming to his feet. "I'll draw. Just let them go and I'll let you show Miss Rutherford how superior you are."

He let the hammer down easy and turned back. His eyebrows arched in question. Thomas had the feeling this man had been rehearsing for this a long, long time. "You must also promise to beg for your life, Thomas. That would be part of our little bargain."

"I agree," Thomas said through clenched teeth, "but first you must let my friends go unharmed."

"They can go."

Thomas motioned for the Crow to run. They hesitated, unwilling to abandon him to face death alone. He was both surprised and then deeply moved by their extraordinary courage and loyalty. He wished he could tell them how grateful he was for this gesture but thought better of it.

What was necessary was to make them go before Pierce changed his mind and decided to kill them. "I said go!" he hissed. "Vamoose! Get the hell out of here!"

He felt like a snake for sounding so angry, but at least they finally decided to return to their horses. When Thomas glanced back along their snowtrail he saw no sign of Moose Mulligan.

The gun barrel stabbed him in the ribs. "Start walking. It's that third tent up ahead, and if you try anything I'll shoot off your kneecaps."

Thomas' mind was operating at a feverish rate. He needed to distract Pierce, rattle him, if at all possible and, if he could, get his hands on the man. "Tell me," he said matter-of-factly, "has it occurred to you that Miss Alice might not want to see me die? That, in fact, she'd rather see *you* die?"

Pierce cursed him softly.

"After all," Thomas continued, wondering if he was about to seal his own death warrant, "she has to realize that you are completely insane."

"Shut up!"

Thomas heard the six-gun cock again. He decided he'd pushed this man about as far as he could without getting himself killed. So he just clamped his mouth shut and kept walking, trying all the while to rub some circulation into his numb fingers so that he could at least hold onto a gun and pull its trigger when the time came to draw.

"I won't kill you cleanly, Thomas. I'm going to put one through your stomach and watch you mess up the snow in your agony."

Thomas tried to blot out the image of himself lying helpless at Pierce's feet, writhing and thrashing about dumb with pain like a shot animal. I must rattle this man just as he is trying to rattle me, Thomas told himself over and over.

He licked his dry lips and his voice came out sounding strained yet clear and mocking. "I heard your family threw you out of Boston. Congratulations, you've just joined me and the rest of my kind in the working class."

"The hell I have! Not after I marry Alice."

Thomas forced a brittle laugh. "She'd never marry a crazy man like you."

The gun barrel smashed down across the back of his head and Thomas grunted in pain and staggered. The pain came in waves, each one larger than the last and threatening to drown out his reason.

Pierce grabbed him by the arm and kept him from pitching into the snow. "You always did have an insolent mouth. As for Miss Alice, I never could stand the way she talked so admiringly about you and how good a man you were with horses. She even told us once that you were better with them than your father!" He snickered. "Thomas, that girl is finally going to see which of us is the real man and which is the coward."

Thomas felt himself being shoved rudely forward. When they reached the tent, Pierce stepped over to the flap and whispered, "Wake up, Miss Rutherford."

She poked her head out almost instantly. When she saw Thomas, she froze with surprise. Thomas thought her just as beautiful as he'd remembered, but now he recognized a hard authority in her that he'd never seen before when she spoke to Pierce. "What are you doing! Let go of him at once!"

"I . . ." He stammered, seemed to grow smaller under her gaze. "I . . . I caught this man trying to steal our horses. He would have left us out here without any way of getting back to Rock Springs."

"Thomas," she asked, turning on him, "is that true?"

"No. I'd have taken the horses, but I'd have returned with them when the buffalo were safe."

"That's a lie!" Pierce choked. "Out West the punishment for horse stealing is death."

She bit her lip, then said, "Get my father."

"No!" Pierce stepped back and his voice pleaded for understanding. "Miss Rutherford, I want to show you how much of a thief and a coward Thomas Atherton really is."

He lowered his voice almost conspiratorially. "You see, I have a special surprise for you. Thomas and I are going to give you a gunfight."

"A what!"

He blinked. The excitement died in his eyes. "A gunfight," he repeated quietly.

"Oh no you aren't," she vowed. "We came West to kill *buffalo*, not Thomas Atherton."

"But. . . ."

She glared up at him. "Please step out of the way. I insist that I speak to my father."

He backed up, his face working with emotion as he tried to comprehend this sudden and unexpected change of events. Then, he stopped and his voice became very still. "You really are in love with him."

"No," she said, finally grasping the real danger. "I never was. He was never more than a valued employee. Nothing more. I swear it!"

"I can't believe you." He began to shake his head back and forth. "You've always led me on. Me and all the others while, inside, you knew you were making fools of us. It was him you wanted all along."

Her cold authority was gone now, replaced by spiraling fear. "That's not true," she insisted with desperation.

But Pierce was all through listening. Thomas watched as he turned away, pushing her out of his life forever. "It doesn't matter," he said hoarsely. "Thomas, draw!"

Because there was no choice at all, he did. His still numbed fingers slapped at the gun at his side even as Pierce's drew level. Suddenly, the familiar boom of Moose Mulligan's big Sharps rifle cut the night air. Franklin Pierce heard the sound, half turned and then was hurled a good ten feet. He crashed over a tent and its poles snapped like bones. Someone inside yelled in confused alarm.

"Run!" Alice shouted. "Run, you stupid fool!"

Thomas tore his eyes away from the dead face of Franklin Pierce. Then, before someone like Cyrus Rutherford killed him, he turned and raced away to save his life.

His legs were on fire and his chest was heaving. Bullets burned across the night, and he felt death on his heels. Up ahead came Moose Mulligan and the Crow Indians with his horse, but he didn't think they'd be able to reach him in time.

Thomas glanced at the moon and saw it had a double ring; he wondered if that was lucky or unlucky. His boots were caked with snow, each step was heavier than the last. He seemed to be running in place.

Now Moose unleashed a wild yell. He was like Zeus astride Pegasus.

"Grab the saddle horn!" Moose yelled. "We'll. . . ."

His mouth formed a circle and out of it came a roar. Pegasus seemed to crash to earth, its body sending diamonds up toward the heavens as a single shot spoke louder and more viciously than all the others from Cyrus Rutherford's big-game hunting rifle.

Moose slammed back in his saddle, dropped his reins and tried to lift his old Sharps buffalo rifle. Up, up it came in his mighty arms until he cradled it to his shoulder, and then Thomas heard that hunting rifle boom again and saw Moose actually rise out of the saddle and be hurled to the snow-covered ground.

Moose was on his back, chest laid open as if he'd taken a cannon ball through the lungs. Yet, somehow, he managed to push the Sharps at Thomas.

"He's your'n, Tom!"

Thomas raised the Sharps. Moose had once shown him how to use it, how to make its bullet streak true across a flat distance to impact with killing force.

Cyrus Rutherford had raced out to stand alone. In the moonlight Thomas could not see his face, yet knew that it was he. Cyrus' perfect rifle, *that* perfect rifle, spoke again and Thomas felt his coat tug him off center. He squared his body to the target, took aim and fired.

The Sharps was eager and ready. Impatient, now it roared in answer. Crude, heavy, almost primitive by comparison, it hurled fire, smoke and lead back at Cyrus. One shot. That was all it had to give and, for a heartbeat, Thomas was certain he'd missed. But then, Rutherford's hands flew up and his rifle spun across the snow. He backpedaled two steps, then toppled to lie still.

When the voice of the buffalo rifle echoed into silence across the snowy hills, Moose seemed to almost pull away from death's hand. His eyes snapped open and burned clear with anticipation.

"Did you kill him?" he whispered.

"Yes."

"Good! I knew you could. We did it, Tom. We saved the buffalo."

Thomas felt as if someone had him by the throat. "You bet we did," he choked.

"The rich girl. Did you see her?"

He nodded.

The fierce old eyes burned up at him. "Do you still want her?"

Thomas smiled. "Hell no. She was always a dream to me. Sally is what's real."

Moose was pleased. His eyes grew soft and rather cloudy. "There's hope for you yet. You'd still make a . . . a good Indian agent. Go back there and bury me . . ." He shuddered. His face drained to a milky white and he almost crushed the bones in Thomas' forearm until the spasm passed. ". . . bury me and my rifle under the buffalo ground. Let 'em stomp and trample over my grave. I owe 'em that . . . much."

He died an instant later, quietly, as if in peace. Thomas shed no tears. He hoped he could live as long and as well as this man.

"Tom!"

It was Sally and she was racing across the land, now throwing herself at his side. But when she saw Moose, what Cyrus' hunting rifle had done to him, she choked in anguish. Thomas held her in his arms. He didn't know how long she cried, but it wasn't until she stopped that he looked up to see Alice Rutherford and the hunting party standing armed and ready. Across from them, the Crow sat their ponies, old rifles poised, also ready.

"Thomas!" Alice Rutherford's voice stung like a whip. "My father is dead."

"So is my friend."

"That man killed Franklin Pierce."

"He deserved—needed—to die." He almost pitied her. "You've come a long way for nothing, Alice."

Her cheeks flamed. "Mount up and get out of here before I have you tried for murder."

"Self-defense," he corrected. "Out West, it happens all the time."

He marveled at her control. Her mouth and eyes moved but the rest of her seemed lifeless, as if she were woodenly playing some role that made no sense yet whose inherited lines she was destined to mouth.

"You *will* leave the buffalo," she told him. "It was my father's. . . ."

"Damn your father!" Sally raged, coming to her feet. "Go back where you came from, Miss Rutherford. And take your dead father and his friends with you!"

Thomas gently laid Moose's head down in the snow and rose to stand beside Sally. He took her hand and found his voice. "God be kind to you, Alice. Now go home and kill your foxes."

Their eyes locked in combat, struggled, and it was hers that finally yielded. Then she turned away and the others followed, muffled footsteps in the snow.

They buried Moose on the reservation, choosing a hillside overlooking the confluence of the Yellowstone and the Big Horn rivers.

In the spring, the buffalo multiplied and Cody's draft for five thousand dollars arrived along with a newspaper article and picture of a fat and very contented Wooly Bully.

With the help of the Reverend Jones and the Crow, Thomas and Sally built a strong, two-room log cabin. One big room for Sally and himself, and a smaller one for their first baby. The Reverend married them with a Bible and then, according to Crow tradition, Tame Doe made Sally a white deerskin wedding dress and braided her hair with feathers. Thomas had never seen a woman so beautiful.

In the bright, wildflowery weeks that followed, they knew they would stay with the Crow as long as they were needed and wanted. And sometimes, right when a sunset bronzed the Montana sky, Thomas and Sally would remark how fine old Moose Mulligan's friendly tombstone lit up the nearby hillside, just like a half-buried crown of gold.